THE HOUSE ON WIDOWS HILL

THE HOUSE ON WIDOWS HILL

Simon R. Green

**SEVERN
HOUSE**

This first world edition published 2020
in Great Britain and the USA by
SEVERN HOUSE PUBLISHERS LTD of
Eardley House, 4 Uxbridge Street, London W8 7SY.
Trade paperback edition first published
in Great Britain and the USA 2021 by
Severn House, an imprint of Canongate Books Ltd,
14 High Street, Edinburgh EH1 1TE.

British Library Cataloguing in Publication Data
A CIP catalogue record for this title is available from the British Library.

ISBN-13: 978-0-7278-9030-6 (cased)
ISBN-13: 978-1-78029-721-7 (trade paper)
ISBN-13: 978-1-4483-0442-4 (e-book)

Typeset by Palimpsest Book Production Ltd.,
Falkirk, Stirlingshire, Scotland.

C all me Ishmael. Ishmael Jones.

In 1963, something new came into the world. From out of the sea of stars, a single lost vessel came howling down through the night skies, its stardrive failing and its superstructure on fire. It crashed in a Wiltshire field, far from anywhere, and the impact killed all of its crew but one. The sole survivor had to be changed by the ship's transformation machines, rewritten as human so it could walk the Earth, unnoticed, until help came. But the machines were damaged in the crash, and they wiped all memories of who and what I used to be, before I was human. I don't even remember where my ship buried itself.

Help never came. I spent decades wandering the Earth as a human among humans, learning by observing, struggling to fit in. I might have thought it was all nothing but a dream or a delusion, except that I haven't aged a day since 1963. I've worked for one underground group after another down the years, because only they possess the necessary resources to hide me from an increasingly suspicious world. Now I work for the Organization, investigating weird cases and strange happenings, in return for guaranteed anonymity.

I should know better than to let anyone get close to me, but these days I have a partner-in-crime, the lovely Penny Belcourt. Because, after all, I'm only human. Together we uncover mysteries, protect people from all manner of unnatural threats and solve the occasional murder.

On the outskirts of the city of Bath, there is a house that no one dares turn their back on. Set high on top of Widows Hill, Harrow House stands alone. Back in Victorian times, something very bad happened there, and the horror of it still lingers. Abandoned for decades, because no one can stand to live in it, Harrow House is not nearly as empty as it should be.

I suppose it's only fitting that a haunted house should end up being investigated by a man haunted by his own past.

ONE

Invitation to a Haunting

I t was the morning after the case before. A politician had been murdered in a toilet locked from the inside, on a moving train, and the suspects involved too many people with secrets and a psychic assassin who wasn't even there. Business as usual, in my line of work. Penny and I found the killer, and handed him over to the authorities when the train arrived at Bath, but by then it was too late to get a train back to London, so we had to spend the night at a hotel.

The Celtic Crown Hotel must have known better days, but I would have been hard pressed to say when. Still, when you arrive around midnight without a reservation or luggage, you have to take what you can get.

Penny and I slept in so late the next morning that when we finally went down for breakfast, the dining area was completely deserted. The staff apparently had more important things to do than wait on us, or even look in occasionally to make sure we weren't stealing the cutlery, so Penny and I just helped ourselves to whatever was left on the hotplates.

I rarely feel up to anything more daunting than a cup of exceedingly black coffee first thing, and I watched with quiet awe as Penny loaded up her plate with a generous sampling of everything on offer. Sausage, bacon, eggs, baked beans, mushrooms and waffles – not so much the Full English as the complete Death by Cholesterol.

Even though all the tables were empty, I'd made a point of choosing one right in the middle of the room, just to make sure no one could sneak up on us without my noticing. The price of security is endless paranoia. I sat quietly, nursing my coffee and waiting for the rest of me to wake up, while Penny attacked the most important meal of her day with cheerful enthusiasm.

She looked really good for someone who'd had to make do with the tiny bottles of generic soap and shampoo supplied by the hotel. A bright young woman with dramatic features, Penny possessed a trim figure, far too much energy for her own good, and a mass of dark hair piled up on top of her head. Her stylish dress of black and white squares currently looked more than a little crumpled, but I wasn't going to be the one to tell her. She caught me studying her and flashed me a dazzling smile.

'I know you don't approve of my choice in breakfasts, darling, but I need to prime the pump a little before I can get stuck into my day.'

'I'm just amazed you could pile so much on to one plate,' I said. 'That's not a meal; it's the leaning tower of sudden heart failure.'

'Given how much the hotel is charging us for our cramped and not even a little bit cosy room, with grey bed sheets and noisy plumbing, I think we're entitled to make the most of our complimentary breakfast,' said Penny. 'Once I'm done with this, I'm going back to check out the cereals and pick up one of every fruit juice they've got.'

'You'll end up rumbling all morning,' I said severely. 'And then want to nap all afternoon.'

She shrugged easily. 'What does it matter? The case is over, and we're on our own time.' And then she stopped and looked at me speculatively. 'I know all of this is bad for *me*, but do you have to worry about things like blocked arteries?'

'Not really,' I said. 'You can't live as long as I have without aging and not suspect the transformation machines made a few improvements on the basic model. My system doesn't even notice things like cholesterol or sugar, and alcohol has never had any effect on me.'

Penny frowned as she stabbed a piece of sausage with her fork before it could get away. 'If the machines made you human so you could fit in, why did they introduce changes that would be bound to make you stand out?'

'I've always assumed the machines were damaged in the crash,' I said.

Penny chewed slowly. 'Unless they did it deliberately.'

'Why would they want to do that?'

'I don't know. Perhaps you should ask the other crash survivor.'

For most of my life I'd believed I was the only one to walk away from the fallen starship, but as a reward for solving our last case in record time, a psychic called Mr Nemo (literally Mr Nobody) had given my memories a nudge and helped me remember that there was another.

My life can get a little weird sometimes, but I've learned to roll with the punches.

'There are a great many things I plan on asking,' I said, 'when I finally track them down. Probably starting with why they've never once reached out to me since we became separated in 1963.'

'All the years you've lived,' said Penny, 'all the things you've done, the people you've helped and the monsters you've faced down . . . It makes my life feel so small, and limited. You walk through the world untouched because you're stronger than anything in it. Everything else just breaks against you.'

'Not everything,' I said. 'You've seen the scars. What brought this on, all of a sudden?'

'How long do you expect to live, Ishmael?' Penny said bluntly. 'How many more years do you think you have in you? How many more than me? You might not age, but I do. What happens when I'm old, and you're . . . still you?'

'I have no idea how long I might live,' I said steadily. 'How could I? But . . . human is as human does. All that matters is that I have every intention of spending the rest of my life with you. However long that turns out to be.'

Penny smiled suddenly. 'You say the sweetest things, darling. If I push you hard enough.'

She attacked her breakfast with renewed enthusiasm while I concentrated on my coffee, thinking my own thoughts. Discovering I wasn't the only one like me in this world had come as something of a shock. If I couldn't trust my earliest memories, what else might I be wrong about? I was sure I was alone when I stumbled away from the crash site, struggling to come to terms with who I suddenly was. So why had my fellow changeling chosen to abandon me?

Finally, Penny cleared her plate, pushed it away and sat back with a satisfied sigh.

'How much do you remember about the second crash survivor, Ishmael?'

I wasn't surprised to find her thoughts had been following mine. That's what makes us such good partners.

'I don't remember their face, or even whether they were male or female. I don't know how we got separated after we left the ship, or why they left me to make my own way in this world for so many years.'

'Maybe they were as confused as you,' said Penny. 'And then . . . couldn't find you again afterwards.'

'Maybe,' I said. 'Or perhaps they actually tracked me down long ago and made themselves a part of my life without saying anything, so they could watch over me until I did remember.'

Penny sat up straight, her eyes widening. 'You think they might be someone you already know? Why wouldn't they have revealed themselves?'

'I don't know,' I said.

Penny frowned. 'What if they've been keeping their distance for a purpose? What if they remember something that you need to be protected from?'

'Then I need to know what that is,' I said.

We both broke off and looked round, as the door to the dining area slammed open and a tall, imposing presence came striding in. Broad-shouldered and barrel-chested, with a gleaming shaven head and skin so dark it had blue highlights, he wore a smart pinstripe suit, white leather gloves and a yellow silk cravat. He was also carrying a large briefcase and heading straight for Penny and me.

'Who is that?' said Penny. 'Do you know him, Ishmael?'

'No,' I said. 'But it looks like he knows us. Which is not the way things are supposed to be.'

The newcomer favoured us with a warm and convivial smile as he drew nearer, but it didn't even come close to touching his eyes. I didn't need to see any ID to know he was one of us. One secret operative can always recognize another; it's something in the way we look at the world, as though we know something no one else does. And usually things no one else would want to know.

I glanced unobtrusively around, checking out how far it was to the other exits, just in case things turned suddenly unpleasant, and so that I could be sure no one else was trying to sneak up on Penny and me while we were distracted.

'He's doing his best to look friendly, but I'm not buying it,' said Penny. 'He's a big man, sweetie; could you take him?'

'Probably,' I said. 'Depends what he has in that briefcase.'

'All right; you knock him over and I'll kick him while he's down.'

'You are a bad influence on me.'

'Everything I know, I learned from watching you and taking notes.'

'Good to know you were paying attention,' I said.

'He must be able to hear what we're saying,' said Penny. 'But he's still heading our way. Which isn't at all ominous. Any idea who this person might be?'

'I recognize the casual arrogance,' I said. 'Clearly an officer type. I wonder who he works for?'

'And why he's come here to bother us on our day off,' said Penny.

The big man never stopped smiling as he wended his way through the maze of tables to join us. He finally came to a halt and inclined his head courteously. 'A very good morning to the both of you, Mr Ishmael Jones and Ms Penny Belcourt! I have the honour to represent the Organization. You may call me Mr Whisper.'

His voice was quiet, little more than a harsh murmur. Some people don't put nearly enough thought into their code names. I eased my chair back from the table, so it wouldn't get in the way if I found it necessary to get to my feet in a hurry. In most fights, it pays to be the one who thinks ahead.

'I only talk to the Colonel,' I said coldly. 'He is my sole point of contact with the Organization. That was the agreement when I first joined.'

'Unfortunately, the Colonel is not currently available,' said Whisper.

'How very convenient,' I said.

'Not particularly, no,' said Whisper. 'But if you would care to consider how your last case ended, with all its various security implications, you'll understand why he's found it necessary to go off the grid and under the radar for a while. I am here in his place, to discuss a matter of some little urgency.'

I studied him thoughtfully. 'You'll understand my caution if I ask for some kind of proof that you really are who and what you say you are.'

'Of course, Mr Jones, of course! I have a mutual acquaintance on my phone right now, just waiting to speak with you. A familiar voice, whose word I believe you will accept without question.'

Whisper produced a mobile phone from inside his jacket and presented it to me with a flourish. I accepted it dubiously and put it to my ear; the psychic Mr Nemo immediately started talking.

'You know who this is. The man who helped you remember you didn't come into this world alone. And no, I haven't told anyone else that – very definitely including the large and forbidding individual standing before you. He is quite definitely a high-up member of the Organization, though how much you trust him is down to you.'

He rang off without giving me a chance to say anything. And it was only after he'd finished talking that I noticed Whisper's phone had never been turned on. Nemo had been speaking directly into my head, which actually went some way to reassure me. Not only that it really was Nemo, but that Whisper hadn't forgotten one of the most basic rules of our profession. Anyone can listen in on a mobile phone these days, and mostly anyone does.

I handed the phone back to Whisper and nodded to Penny.

'That was Nemo. He vouches for Whisper.'

'You should have told him I said hi!'

'He's psychic,' I said. 'He probably already knew.'

I turned my attention back to Whisper.

'All right,' I said. 'You're the real deal. What do you want?'

'Given that the Organization is responsible for us being stranded in Bath overnight, perhaps he's come to pay our hotel bill?' Penny said sweetly.

'That has already been taken care of, dear lady,' said Whisper.

I fixed him with a hard look. 'How did you know to find us here? I didn't tell anyone where we were staying.'

Whisper showed me his meaningless smile again. 'The Organization always knows where you are, Mr Jones. You are, after all, one of our most valuable assets.'

'I don't think I like the sound of that,' I said.

'How else can we protect you, Mr Jones?'

'I can look after myself.'

'Only if you see them coming.'

'Why are you dressed like that?' Penny said suddenly. 'For a secret agent, you're not exactly blending in.'

'When I dress this way, people only remember the outfit,' Whisper said comfortably. 'This is merely what I look like today. Tomorrow, I will look like someone else. Now, I am here to ask you and your partner to take on a new assignment.'

I glared at him. 'We are guaranteed proper downtime between missions! I've seen too many good agents burn out from trying to take on too much, and I'm not going to let that happen to Penny and me.'

'Normally, that would, of course, be the proper procedure,' said Whisper. 'But this is not a normal case. If I might be permitted to sit down and explain?'

I nodded reluctantly. Whisper pulled a chair over from the next table and sat down opposite Penny and me. Up close, he looked even larger and a great deal more solid. I half expected the chair to collapse under his weight. Whisper folded his white-gloved hands on the table in front of him and fixed me with a steady gaze.

'Is this another emergency?' said Penny, before he could even start. 'We've only just finished dealing with the last one. And why does it always have to be us? Doesn't the Organization have anyone else they can call on?'

'Of course, dear lady,' said Whisper. 'But I do not talk about them, any more than I talk about you.'

'Well, that's good to know,' I said. 'I'm not committing myself to anything, but . . . What's so important about this case?'

'Indeed, indeed, Mr Jones, let us immerse ourselves in the

business at hand, and not use up any more of the time that is fast slipping away.' Whisper leaned forward conspiratorially. 'This new assignment is not an official emergency, as such, but your assistance is most urgently required. You are being offered this case simply because you are here. No one else is even close. Please believe me when I say that you should in no way consider yourselves under any pressure or obligation to agree; this particular case should be seen as more of a personal favour. The Organization would like you to investigate a supposedly haunted house, right here in Bath, and determine what is really going on there. The name of this unfortunate residence is Harrow House. Perhaps you've heard of it?'

I glanced at Penny, and she shook her head quickly.

'Should we know it?' I said.

'I am told the haunted house on Widows Hill is spoken of most respectfully, among those with an interest in such matters,' said Whisper.

'Ghosts aren't really our territory,' said Penny.

'Right,' I said. 'We investigate mysteries and security problems. We don't deal in things that go *boo!* in the night.'

Whisper nodded solemnly. His dark face remained completely impassive, but I thought I detected a certain embarrassment in his body language.

'It seems that a certain high-up member of the Organization was planning to buy a house here in Bath. He thought he'd found exactly what he was looking for, but the price turned out to be so low that it aroused his suspicions, and when he questioned the estate agents, they were forced to admit that Harrow House has a long history of being very seriously haunted.'

I had to raise an eyebrow. 'And this high-up member of the Organization actually believes in things like that?'

Whisper met my gaze unflinchingly. 'He is often required to believe in stranger things. It comes with the job. Your assignment, should you choose to accept it, is to check out and confirm the true nature of the house before he commits to buying it.'

I was already shaking my head. 'I'm not the one you need for something like this. I don't even believe in ghosts.'

'All the better, Mr Jones!' Despite Whisper's apparent enthusiasm, his voice never once rose above the rough murmur that gave him his name. 'A sceptical mind is exactly what is required here. The gentleman in question wants nothing more than to be reassured that this is all nonsense. Apparently, he feels the need for hard evidence to back this up, from someone he can trust.'

I grinned at Penny. 'What are the odds it'll all turn out to be just the caretaker in a scary mask, frightening everyone off so he can concentrate on searching for the hidden treasure?'

'And he'd have gotten away with it too, if it hadn't been for us pesky investigators,' Penny said solemnly.

'I think we would all be happy to settle for such an outcome,' said Whisper.

I leaned back in my chair and looked at him thoughtfully. 'Why hasn't the Organization reached out to one of the underground groups who specialize in these matters?'

'Hold it right there! Stop the car and throw on the handbrake,' said Penny. 'There really are such groups? That's a thing – an actual thing?'

'So I am assured,' said Whisper.

'It takes all sorts,' I said.

'You should know, Mr Jones,' said Whisper.

'But if there are such groups, does that mean ghosts definitely are real?' said Penny.

'The answer to that question is most certainly outside my area of expertise,' Whisper said carefully.

'And what area would that be?' I said.

Whisper flashed me another empty smile. 'I am no more inclined to discuss the secrets of my life than you are concerning your own, Mr Jones. Now, if we could please concentrate on the matter before us . . . It is vital that this delicate business is sorted out as quickly as possible, before other groups in our line of business discover what's happening and start spreading the news.'

'That a high-up member of the Organization is scared he might have spooks in his belfry?' I said.

'That he might be in danger of being taken advantage of,' said Whisper.

I looked at Penny. 'And that's why he didn't reach out to the so-called experts. He can't afford to be seen as indecisive – or gullible. Perception of strength is everything where security is concerned.'

'Exactly, Mr Jones!' said Whisper. 'You have embraced the essence of the situation in a nutshell.'

'You still haven't made it clear why I should agree to get involved in such a dubious case,' I said.

Whisper paused, choosing his words with great care. 'I have been instructed to assure you that your accepting this assignment will be regarded as a personal favour, both to the individual himself and to the Organization. In return, they are prepared to grant you a favour. Anything you want, apparently . . . Within reason, of course.'

I smiled slowly. 'Your timing couldn't be better, Mr Whisper. I could use some assistance in tracking down a very hard-to-find individual. This isn't connected to any current Organization case, but the person concerned is someone with a lot of experience when it comes to hiding from people like us.'

'I don't see any problem there,' said Whisper. 'I am sure the Organization will be only too happy to place all its resources at your disposal. Once you've got to the bottom of whatever it is that's going on at Harrow House.'

'And no questions asked?'

'Of course, Mr Jones, that is both implicit and understood. So, do we have an understanding?'

I turned to Penny. 'What do you think? Do you feel up to taking on another case so soon after the last one?'

'Are you kidding?' said Penny, all but bouncing up and down on her seat. 'I've watched every haunted house movie there is, including the comedies. I've always wanted to have a crack at investigating a real one!'

'All right, then,' I said. 'Just for you.' I nodded to Whisper. 'We'll do it.'

'Splendid!' said Whisper. 'I have assembled all the information you will need to get you started.'

He set his briefcase down on the table, opened the lock with a flourish and pulled out a large manila folder. He patted it approvingly with one large white-gloved hand and then pushed the file across the table.

'This contains full details on Harrow House, including its troubled history and all the extraordinary stories currently associated with it. Please make yourselves familiar with the information as quickly as possible . . . because the Organization has already arranged for you to spend the night at Harrow House. Starting at eight o'clock this evening.'

I considered the sheer size and weight of the file. 'How much of this is actually relevant?'

'That is for you to decide, Mr Jones,' said Whisper. 'Now . . . I'm afraid I do have some bad news to share with you.'

I gave him my best raised eyebrow. 'Why did I just know you were going to say that?'

'Years of experience, I should think,' said Whisper. 'It will, unfortunately, be necessary for you to work alongside a small group of fellow investigators into the unknown. All of them amateurs, but each and every one a specialist in their own chosen field. The high-up member of the Organization was most insistent that he wanted all the angles covered.'

'Angles?' I said suspiciously. 'What else is there, apart from simple logic and common sense?'

'Alternative viewpoints,' Whisper said smoothly. 'You said it yourself, Mr Jones: this isn't your area of expertise. Everything you need to know about your new colleagues can be found in the file. Now, you will be required to spend the entire night on the premises, whatever happens – until our people come to pick you up first thing in the morning. At which point, Mr Jones, you and Ms Belcourt will make your determination known directly to me, and only to me.'

'We only get one night to make up our minds?' I said.

'I have been assured that one night is all you will need,' said Whisper.

Penny clapped her hands delightedly. 'Oh, this is going to be such fun!'

While I was looking at her, Whisper got to his feet. 'Allow me to wish both of you the very best of luck. Given some of the more disturbing tales associated with Harrow House, it would seem likely that you're going to need it. I will meet with you again tomorrow morning. Assuming you survive the night, of course.'

He chuckled richly, inclined his large head to both of us, turned with magisterial grace and strode back out of the dining area. The door closed silently and very firmly behind him.

'At least we got our hotel bill paid,' said Penny.

'I am not happy about having to work with Team Ghost,' I said. 'I do not play well with others.'

'I have noticed that,' said Penny. 'And Ishmael . . . I have to say I'm really not sure that getting the Organization involved in your search for the other crash survivor is such a great idea. I mean, how much can you safely tell them, without putting yourself in danger?'

'It's a risk I have to take,' I said. 'I need the kind of resources a big organization can throw at the problem. They can cover a lot of ground, and get answers from the kind of people who would never open up to someone like me. And . . . the Organization was able to find me, originally – at a time when I didn't think anyone could. Who better, then, to locate someone like me?'

'But what can you tell them?'

'I can give them the date the ship crashed and the general area,' I said. 'Then ask them to search for weird happenings associated with that, and see where it takes us.'

Penny shook her head. 'They're bound to get suspicious about why you want to know.'

'They're always suspicious,' I said. 'I just hope I'm valuable enough to the Organization that they won't want to risk scaring me off.'

Penny nodded reluctantly and turned her attention to the file.

'How do you want to approach this? You've always been very emphatic that there are no such things as ghosts. Even though our previous cases have seen us going up against vampires, werewolves and psychics.'

'That's different,' I said.

'How?'

'They're all to do with the living. The science may be a bit extreme, but it's still part of the real world. Paranormal, as opposed to supernatural. Do you believe in ghosts? I mean, honestly?'

'I've never seen one,' said Penny. 'But I'm intrigued by the possibility.'

I shook my head firmly. 'Once you start accepting the existence of things like ghosts, where do you stop? I'm prepared to accept the phenomenon: that people see things they take for ghosts. Images of people, and places, from the past. But that could be down to stone tape recordings, psychic impressions, timeslips . . . All of them more than a little unlikely, but a lot easier to believe than that the dead sometimes return to walk among the living. Dead is dead. In fact, given the sheer number of appalling people I have found it necessary to do away with down the years, they'd better stay dead or I could be in serious trouble.'

'Let's see what the file has to say,' Penny said diplomatically.

She moved her chair in beside me, and we worked our way through the pages together.

Harrow House had apparently been the scene of many unpleasant stories, dating all the way back to Victorian times. And yet I couldn't find any reports of sightings of actual ghosts. No dim figures walking through walls, or staring out of mirrors, or standing at the foot of someone's bed in the early hours. Nothing that could even pass for poltergeist activity. I said as much to Penny, and she looked at me amusedly.

'For someone who doesn't believe in ghosts, you seem to know an awful lot about the subject.'

'I have read the occasional book,' I said. 'Just out of curiosity.'

Penny nodded understandingly and turned back to the file.

'I'm not seeing any of the background stories you'd expect from any respectable haunted house. No unsolved murders, no strange disappearances, not even a suicide . . . Ghosts don't just come from nowhere.'

I leafed through the remaining pages, glancing ahead. 'Why is everyone so convinced Harrow House is haunted, when no one's reported seeing anything that could even pass for a restless spirit?'

Penny pulled the file away from me and turned back to where we'd stopped.

'The one thing everyone describes is an overwhelming sense of dread and horror that affects anyone who stays in the house. Feelings so unbearable that they literally drive people out. That's why the place has remained empty for so long. Look at this report, from 1927: "The house was full of horror, and a sense of death. I honestly felt that I would die if I stayed. Some terrible voice seemed to be warning me to get out while I still could. There is a spirit inhabiting Harrow House, and it is not human." No wonder the local community won't go anywhere near it.'

'Most of these stories come from local people,' I said. 'Usually youngsters, whose curiosity took them too close to the house. Tales of lights blazing in windows, when the house was known to be empty. Strange sounds from inside, which might have been voices, though no one could understand what they were saying. All very spooky, I'm sure, but you don't need a supernatural presence to explain things like that.'

Penny nodded slowly. 'The only thing that everyone seems to agree on is the awful way the house makes people feel.' She sat back in her chair and looked at me. 'Well, what do you think?'

I did Penny the courtesy of taking her question seriously and gave the matter some thought.

'If you believe you're in a bad place, you're bound to get bad feelings,' I said finally. 'All the people who entered or even approached the house did so expecting to be scared. Jumping at every moving shadow or unexpected sound. I think Harrow House is probably nothing more than a really big Rorschach inkblot, where everyone sees what they expect to see, and feels what they've been told they'll feel. Once we get in there, it shouldn't take us long to prove that nothing out of the ordinary is going on. We won't be so easily frightened, because we're used to facing real threats.'

'Assuming Team Ghost doesn't get in the way,' said Penny. 'They're bound to have their own ideas as to what's happening.'

I nodded grimly. 'Let's see what the file has to say about these people.'

There were individual reports on all four amateur experts, including a number of clippings from the local press. Someone at the Organization had gone out of their way to do a thorough job.

Lynn Barrett was a celebrity psychic who specialized in cleansing haunted houses. How much she charged for this service wasn't made clear. I studied the publicity photo provided; she looked every inch the glamorous professional. Apart from the heavy Goth makeup and a definite propensity for the dramatic pose.

'A psychic,' said Penny. 'Like the one we met yesterday?'

'I very much doubt it,' I said. 'Mr Nemo was a member of the British Psychic Weapons Group. Lynn Barrett is just a self-appointed miracle-worker; only one step up from reading tea leaves and telling people they've got a lucky face. What does cleansing a house mean, anyway? That could involve anything from feng shui to aromatherapy.'

'I'm guessing you don't believe in those, either,' said Penny.

'I'd believe in ghosts first,' I said. 'At least she doesn't call herself a medium. They're never anything more than confidence tricksters, using cold reading techniques to separate the vulnerable from their life savings.'

'By any chance, did you have a bad experience?'

'Keep reading,' I said.

Tom Shaw was an amateur ghost-chaser, who spent all his spare time searching for evidence of life after death using special scientific equipment.

'You've got that look on your face again,' said Penny. 'Stop frowning, before you give yourself wrinkles.'

'Using science to look for ghosts,' I said, 'is like using a telescope to look for angels.'

'There's quite a lot of clippings about him,' said Penny, leafing quickly through them. 'It does look as if he's tried to help people . . . And at least he seems to be putting his faith in technology, rather than just holding hands in the dark and asking if there's anybody there.'

'What kind of tech does he use?' I said.

Penny got to the end of the clippings and shook her head. 'Doesn't say. Probably motion detectors, instruments to measure changes in room temperature or electromagnetic anomalies.' She shot me a quick grin. 'I have also been known to read the occasional book on the subject.'

Tom Shaw didn't bother with promotional photos, but images from the local press showed a stocky middle-aged man, frowning purposefully as he pointed some unfamiliar device at a likely shadow.

'I thought you'd approve of someone who put his faith in science,' said Penny.

'I don't think I'd call what he does science,' I said.

'Snob,' said Penny.

Arthur Welles was a reporter for a local newspaper, the *Bath Herald*. The only photo looked as if it came from his driving licence, and showed a young man with a serious face, scowling at a world that was always going to disappoint him by never being what he wanted it to be. Just starting out in his chosen career, and more than ready to tackle the kind of stories his more experienced colleagues couldn't be bothered with. According to the file, he'd insisted on being involved in Team Ghost because his family owned Harrow House.

And, finally, there was Winifred Stratton. No press clippings, no photo, just basic biographical data and a list of self-published books she'd written.

'It says here that she's a local historian and a white witch,' said Penny. 'Two for the price of one. Author of such volumes as *The History They Don't Tell You About*, *Making Friends With Ghosts* and *Your Hidden Powers*.'

I shook my head slowly. 'Oh, this can only go well.'

TWO

It Isn't Just a House

That evening, a taxi from the Organization appeared outside the hotel, to take us to Harrow House. I opened the door for Penny, and she arranged herself grandly on the back seat like a film star on her way to a premiere. I got in beside her, and the driver turned all the way round in his seat to give us his best welcoming smile. A large middle-aged man in a crumpled jacket, he addressed us with a broad local accent and seemed genuinely pleased to have us in his cab.

'Welcome, sir and madam! My name is Dennis, and I will be your chauffeur for tonight. My dad always said drive like a chauffeur, which I always took to mean drive like you're sleeping with the boss's wife. For the amount of money that's already been paid in advance, including your extremely generous tip, I am more than happy to take you anywhere you might want to go in our wonderful city.

'So, what's your pleasure, madam and sir? The theatre, the opera . . . I know all the best restaurants and clubs . . . Or perhaps you'd prefer somewhere exotic, like Spearmint Rhino or Burlesque Babes? And, of course, if your tastes run to the more extreme diversions, I can always recommend some very discreet establishments where everyone is guaranteed not to remember your name . . .'

'Take us to Harrow House, on Widows Hill,' I said.

Dennis's smile didn't so much disappear as die by inches. He looked from me to Penny and then back again, as though giving us a chance to change our minds; when he saw that wasn't going to happen, he just nodded curtly and turned away.

'I should have known the money was too good,' he said, the professional cheer completely gone from his voice. 'If I'd known that was where you wanted to go, I would have phoned in sick this morning and hidden under the bed till it was over.'

'You know about Harrow House?' said Penny.

'Everyone in this city does,' said Dennis. 'Though most of them have enough sense not to talk about it to outsiders. An American film director came here a few years back, looking to make some kind of documentary, and he couldn't even find anyone who'd admit to having heard of the place. Trust me, it's not somewhere anyone should want to go.'

'We do,' I said. 'We have business there.'

Dennis revved his engine and sent the taxi roaring out into the flow of traffic. He didn't bother to check his satnav; he knew where Harrow House was. After driving for a while in silence, he glowered at Penny and me in his rear-view mirror.

'Why would you want to go to that awful place?' he said roughly, as though he felt compelled to ask. 'What reason could possibly be good enough to take you to that little piece of hell on earth?'

'We represent someone who's thinking of buying it,' said Penny.

Dennis looked as though he wanted to laugh, but his heart wasn't in it. 'Lots of people have thought about buying Harrow House. I'm told the price is very tempting. But all it takes is one good look and then they all decide they'd be better off looking somewhere else. I've driven people to the top of Widows Hill before, and not one of them ever thanked me for it.'

'We'll be fine,' I said. 'We don't scare easily.'

'You've never been to Harrow House,' said Dennis. 'Whoever you represent, tell them the only good reason to buy that place would be to burn it down and then piss on the ashes.'

'You sound scared,' said Penny.

'That's probably because I am.'

'Why?' I said.

'Because it isn't just a house. It's supposed to be empty, but it isn't. There's something in it.'

'What kind of something?' said Penny.

'No one knows,' said Dennis. 'And no one wants to know.'

He drove on, staring straight ahead and saying nothing. The traffic gradually thinned out, and by the time we reached the outskirts of the city, we had the road almost entirely to ourselves. The last of the light was dropping out of the day, and the street lamps glowed bravely, holding back the dark. Out on the edge of the city, the whole area had an empty, abandoned feel, as though most people had the good sense to be somewhere else. Dennis suddenly started talking again.

'It's always a bad idea to go poking around Harrow House. Nothing good ever comes of it.'

'You still haven't explained why,' said Penny, in her most winning voice. 'Ishmael and I have investigated more than our fair share of houses with bad reputations. We know how to look after ourselves.'

'You've never seen anything like Harrow House,' said Dennis. 'No one has. It's not a spooky story for tourists; that house destroys people. The locals won't go anywhere near it.'

'Any particular reason?' I said, trying not to sound too pointed.

'Because they know better,' said Dennis. 'There's nothing like living close to a predator to sharpen your survival instincts.'

His gaze met mine in the rear-view mirror, checking me out to see whether I was ready to take him seriously. I did my best to appear receptive and trustworthy. Dennis sighed heavily. He sounded more resigned than reassured, but finally he took a deep breath and launched into his story. Wherever there's a haunted house, there's always someone with a story.

'I've heard of people who went into Harrow House and never came out again. When friends or neighbours went in to look for them, keeping close together for their own protection, they couldn't find a trace of the missing people anywhere. There are other stories, about strange lights that come and go in the house's windows, and doors that aren't always there. People have heard voices crying out in the night, while local pets are always being found dead outside the house gates, without a mark on them. And birds just drop dead out of the sky.'

Penny and I exchanged a glance. A lot of this was almost word for word what we'd read in Mr Whisper's file.

'These voices,' said Penny. 'What do they say?'

'Everyone hears something different,' said Dennis. 'Half the time it's not even a language anyone recognizes. Which is strange, given that there are all kinds living in the area around Widows Hill. Not because they want to; it's just all they can afford. Harrow House poisons that whole area, just by being there. And once . . .'

He broke off and had to swallow hard before he could continue. When he did start speaking again, something in his voice made me lean forward in my seat so I wouldn't miss anything.

'Back when I was just a kid,' Dennis said slowly, 'twelve years old and ready to take on the whole world, I used to be part of this gang. Just a bunch of kids from school, but at that age who doesn't want to be in a gang? Our leader was Kevin – the oldest of us, and the bravest. Always ready to lead us into anything that looked like it might be fun. And if it was something we weren't supposed to be doing, all the better. We got into a lot of trouble, but that was just part of the fun.

'It was the Fifth of November, Guy Fawkes' Night. We'd all told our parents we were going to one of the big organized fireworks displays, but we had something far more exciting in mind. We were going to pay a visit to the haunted house on Widows Hill. It was a rite of passage for all the local children back then: to go to the house and look through the locked gates. Prove that you were so brave that not even its reputation could keep you away. Of course, no one ever tried to open the gates and go inside. It was enough to prove your courage by looking at the house, and then running away.

'But that night . . . we didn't stop at the gates.'

He broke off again. I studied Dennis's face in the rear-view mirror. He looked honestly troubled by what he was remembering, despite all the years that had passed. He stayed quiet for so long that I began to wonder if he'd said all he was going to, or at least all he could bring himself to talk about, but suddenly he started up again. As though he couldn't help but tell it all, now that he'd started.

'It was a quiet night. The odd explosion of colour lit up the skies, but the fireworks were so far off we couldn't hear them. The streets were empty. No one about. No one to challenge us as to where we were going. We walked all the way up Widows Hill, and though we were joking and laughing when we started, there wasn't a word out of any of us by the time we got to the top and stood outside the gates to Harrow House. We crowded in together and peered curiously through the spiked iron bars.

'The grounds were heavily overgrown, with trees and hedges and all kinds of things that had been left to their own devices for far too long. All of it packed so close together they were fighting each other for room to breathe. I'm told it used to be a very elegant and formal garden, laid out in pleasant patterns, once upon a time . . . but it had been left to run riot for so long that now it was just a great green mess. The old pathways were choked with hanging branches and thorny vines. But one path was still open, leading straight to the house's front door.

'There were no lights showing in any of the windows that night, no strange sounds or voices. Nothing out of the ordinary – just an old house standing alone, surrounded by a garden no one cared about any more. Nothing to scare us, but we were scared, all the same. Just the sight of Harrow House was enough to put a chill in our hearts.

'But having come this far, and got this close, none of us were prepared to admit what we were feeling. We were Kevin's gang, the bravest of the brave and the boldest of the bold, always ready to do what no other kid would. So we pressed up against the black iron bars, to see as much as we could. So we could boast about it afterwards, to our admiring peers.

'I don't know what got into us, but suddenly we were daring each other to open the gates and go in. None of us thought the gates would actually open, of course; everyone knew they were kept locked. It was all about daring each other to try. And, of course, in the end, Kevin did. I thought he'd just rattle the bars a little and that would be that, honour satisfied. But the gates opened immediately at his touch. Swinging slowly back, without a single creak from the hinges, as though opening was something they did every day.

'No one was ever sure whether the gates were locked to keep people out or something else in. No one ever visited Harrow House without special permission. Caretakers were supposed to go in every six months, to make sure everything was as it should be, but even they had to be hired from firms outside the city, because no one local would do it for any amount of money. Harrow House was a sleeping beast that no one wanted to awaken.

'We looked at the gates that should never have opened, and then at each other. None of us wanted to go in. But when Kevin finally stepped forward, we all had to follow him, of course. Because he was our leader.

'The grounds seemed awfully still, as though everything in the garden had stopped what it was doing to watch us. The light from the street lamps couldn't get past the high stone walls surrounding the property, but moonlight shimmered the whole length of the gravel path that led to the front door of Harrow House. Slumping hedges and swaying branches pressed right up against the edges of the path, but they never once crossed its borders, as though something wanted that path left open, for poor damned fools like us.

'Kevin strode along the path with his head held high, making straight for the house. He never hesitated once. And we were all so proud of him; we were right behind him, backing him up. Our shoes crunched loudly on the gravel, as though announcing we were on our way. We stuck close together, shoulders bumping against shoulders, our eyes fixed on the front door. I kept expecting someone to say we'd done enough, that we'd already dared far more than any other kid ever had, so it would be all right for us to just turn around and leave. But none of us even suggested it. At that age you're more afraid of what your friends might say than any haunted house.

'We left the gates behind, following the path through the shapeless masses of greenery, whatever form or function they might have had long since lost and forgotten. I remember there weren't any flowers, not a touch of colour anywhere, and the shadows were all so dark and so deep. Harrow House loomed up before us, growing steadily larger and more imposing. And the dark windows stared at us like so many empty eyes.

'We finally stopped before the front door. It was shut, just as it was supposed to be, and we stood there for a long moment

like carol singers who'd forgotten all their songs. The door
was huge, at least twice our height, a massive slab of dark
wood. Smooth and blank and very solid, more like a barrier
than an entrance. There was no electric bell, no iron knocker
on the door – just an old-fashioned bell-chain, hanging
down. None of us wanted to touch it, not even Kevin, for fear
of what it might summon. But we didn't need to. The door
opened on its own.

'There was no sound of a lock turning, no creak or groan
from the hinges. The door just fell slowly back before us,
as though inviting us in. Beyond it, there was nothing to see
but the dark. A darkness so complete anything could have
been hiding inside it, anything at all.

'I don't remember which of us broke first, but suddenly
we were all sprinting back down the path. My heart was
pounding so hard it felt like it might leap out of my chest at
any moment. I kept my gaze fixed on the gates, convinced
they were going to swing shut at the last moment, and we'd
end up pressed helplessly against the black iron bars, struggling desperately to get out . . . while something from inside
the house slouched unhurriedly down the path to get us. And
I thought that if something so much as placed a hand on my
shoulder, I would die from sheer horror. But the gates didn't
close, and we ran through them and straight on down the hill.

'I was the only one who hesitated and looked back, to see
the front door of Harrow House slowly close. As though it
was disappointed. And then I was off and running down
Widows Hill with the rest of them, and none of us stopped
running until we were safely home.'

Dennis stopped talking, and silence filled the cab. All the
time he'd been telling us about this terrible thing from his
childhood, he'd been driving his taxi through the streets quite
calmly and professionally, but his voice had grown steadily
quieter, as though just talking about what had happened had
taken all the strength out of him. Penny and I said nothing,
giving him the time he needed to compose himself.

'We never told anybody what we'd done,' he said finally.
'Our parents would have given us a good hiding for being so
stupid, and we couldn't admit to anyone at school that we'd

run away. We never even discussed it among ourselves, prefer-
ring to pretend it never happened. That was the end of Kevin
and his gang. We didn't want to be around each other any
more, after that.'

'If you never told anyone before,' I said carefully, 'why are
you telling us now?'

'Because you need to know,' said Dennis. 'That house is a
bad place. Bad things happen there.'

His face in the rear-view mirror was unhealthily pale and
beaded with sweat. His mouth had set in a grim line, as though
to make sure he couldn't tell us anything else. Penny and I looked
at each other. The first few stories he'd told us had sounded
pretty generic, just traditional friend-of-a-friend stuff, but his
personal account had sounded much more like the real thing.

Dennis swung the taxi round in a sudden sharp turn, and,
just like that, we were roaring up a steep hill. I didn't need
to glimpse the battered sign on an old stone wall to know
we'd reached Widows Hill. We passed several old houses along
the way, all set some distance apart and standing well back
from the road. None of them had any lights showing. The
street lamps grew further apart, and their light took on a sickly,
unwholesome look.

'It's not too late,' said Dennis, staring straight ahead. 'I
can always turn around at the top and drive you back to
your hotel.'

'No,' I said. 'We can't do that. We're here to do a job.'

'Don't worry, Dennis,' said Penny. 'We'll be careful.'

'We know what we're doing,' I said.

Dennis had nothing more to say, all the way up the hill. He
finally brought his taxi to a halt some distance short of the
high stone walls surrounding Harrow House, and even after
he'd stopped, he kept his engine running. He wouldn't glance
at us in his rear-view mirror; it was as though he'd already
written us off. He just sat there, refusing even to look in the
house's direction, waiting for us to get out of his cab. We
stepped out into the cool air of the evening, and Dennis
immediately turned his taxi around in a tight arc and shot off
down the hill, accelerating all the way, back to the safety of
the streets he trusted.

Penny and I walked over to the tall gates, the only break in the featureless stone walls surrounding the property. The spiked black iron bars looked strong and sturdy. Made to keep the world out or hold something else in. I deliberately turned my back on the gates and looked out at the view over Bath. From the top of Widows Hill the brightly lit streets of the city lay spread out before me, looking so far away they might have been another world. A blaze of light, defying the darkness. Penny moved in beside me and slipped her arm through mine.

'I think we'd better ask the Organization to send its own car to pick us up in the morning.'

'I have to wonder why they hired a taxi at all,' I said. 'And why they chose Dennis to be our driver. Did they know what had happened to him, and wanted him to tell us?'

'That does sound like something they'd do,' said Penny.

We turned back to the gates, taking our time, to show we weren't in any way impressed or intimidated, and peered through the bars at Harrow House. Alone and isolated, it had been built at the very top of the hill, its nearest neighbours some distance away. Cut off from people and the rest of the city – presumably by choice. The gates had no particular style or ornamentation; they'd been designed to be strictly functional. A barrier between the house and the world.

But tonight someone had left them standing ajar. Almost invitingly.

'It does seem like we're expected,' I said.

'You say that as though it's a good thing,' said Penny.

I raised an eyebrow. 'Are you having second thoughts, now you're faced with an actual haunted house?'

'I did think it would be more fun,' Penny admitted. 'But just looking at Harrow House makes my skin crawl. It feels like being watched, by a monster in a cave. Where's the Scooby Gang when you need them?'

I pushed the gates all the way open and we walked through, into the grounds. Which turned out to be an even greater mess than Dennis had described, the rioting greenery more like a jungle than a garden. But the single gravel path leading to the house was still completely clear, an open way to where

Harrow House stood waiting for us. A large blocky Victorian pile, grim and dark and brooding, it had the look of one of those old mansions you used to see on the covers of Gothic romance novels. The kind you just knew weren't going to end well.

'I can't say I'm impressed,' I said finally. 'It's just a house.'

'But it does have an atmosphere,' said Penny, frowning. 'As though there's more to it than just a house.'

'I'm not feeling anything,' I said firmly.

Penny shrugged, almost angrily. 'I'm picking up . . . something. But that could just be me.'

'Perhaps the full dread and horror doesn't kick in until we're actually inside the house,' I said.

'Then let's go check it out,' Penny said firmly. 'I am just in the mood to kick some supernatural arse.'

'Never knew you when you weren't,' I said gallantly.

We set off along the gravel path. And if Penny's arm pressed a little more tightly against mine, neither of us said anything. There were no lights showing in any of the house's windows, but a small group of people were standing together before the closed front door. They watched us approach in silence.

'Oh, good,' I said. 'Team Ghost are here to welcome us.'

'Give them a chance,' Penny said sternly. 'They might know all sorts of useful things.'

'And if not, we can always use them as human shields.'

'You're so practical, darling,' said Penny.

She waved cheerfully to the waiting group with her free arm, but not one of them responded.

'Not exactly friendly, are they?' said Penny, her eyes narrowing just a bit dangerously.

'For all we know, they might be the ghosts of Harrow House,' I said.

Penny sniffed. 'I can't help feeling real ghosts would put on more of a show.'

We continued along the gravel path, deliberately not hurrying. It wasn't as though I was looking forward to meeting Team Ghost. A celebrity psychic, a ghostbuster, a white witch and a reporter . . . I was having a hard time deciding which of them was most likely to get on my nerves first.

'Play nicely with our new colleagues, sweetie,' Penny murmured. 'We have to get along with these people if we're going to make any progress.'

'I think they should put some effort into getting along with us,' I said. 'If only because we're far more likely to get to the bottom of whatever's going on here than any of them.'

'So you do think something is going on?'

'I don't like the feel of the house,' I admitted. 'As though it's hiding something from us.'

'Are you feeling anything specific?'

'Nothing I can put a name to. Not dread or horror, just . . . a general feeling of being watched, by unseen eyes.'

'I am definitely feeling all of that,' said Penny.

'Remember the ink blot,' I said. 'It's more than likely we're only feeling these things because the file told us we would.'

'But we're professionals,' said Penny. 'You are space boy, I am spy girl; we're used to walking into dangerous situations. *We* don't get nervous; we make other people nervous. And yet . . . it does feel as if something in that house is waiting for us, and rubbing its hands together in anticipation.'

I had to smile. 'Like we're walking into a trap?'

Penny grinned and squeezed my arm against her side. 'Nothing new there, darling. In fact, that's pretty much our job description.'

'One supernatural arse-kicking coming right up,' I said cheerfully.

We finally reached the small group of people standing before the door. They looked more impatient than scared, and didn't make any move to greet us; they just studied Penny and me with open suspicion. So I made a point of giving all of them my most charming smile.

'Good evening to one and all,' I said. 'I am Ishmael Jones, and this is my partner, Penny Belcourt. We are here to represent the party interested in buying this property, who for the time being prefers to remain anonymous.'

'Why can't you tell us their name? Is there some reason why we aren't allowed to know?' The interrogation came from a surly young man in faded jeans and a shabby Black Sabbath T-shirt. He was tall and gangling, with a face that was trying for character when it should have settled for handsome. 'I'm Arthur Welles, reporter for the *Bath Herald.*'

'Shouldn't you already know the buyer's name?' Penny said sweetly. 'After all, it's your family that's selling this not particularly desirable property.'

Arthur scowled. 'According to them, the sale was arranged entirely through intermediaries. Which, of course, isn't the least bit suspicious.'

'There are security aspects to the buyer's identity,' I said smoothly. 'Which is why he prefers to keep his identity secret, for the moment.'

Arthur perked up at that and looked ready to launch into a whole new series of questions, so I turned away to meet the others.

I sort of recognized Lynn Barrett from her publicity photo. The celebrity house-cleanser was actually a tiny little thing, barely five feet tall, wearing a black dress that managed to be both severe and stylish. Her shoulder-length hair was equally dark, and her face was almost buried under industrial-strength Goth makeup: pale skin, black lips, so much mascara and heavy false eyelashes I was amazed she could see anything through them. Surprisingly, her fingernails had been painted a shocking pink. She carried a heavy wicker bag slung over one shoulder, and clutched it to her protectively.

'I'm Lynn Barrett. Spiritual advocate,' she said, in a soft but compelling voice. She favoured me with a warm but mysterious smile, which she probably practised every day in front of a mirror. 'Your connection between everyday life and all the wonders of the hidden world.'

'How nice for you,' I said.

Her smile widened. 'Ah . . . a sceptic. Good. I enjoy converting people like you. I love the way they thank me afterwards for opening their minds to the truth.'

I smiled back at her. 'Not going to happen.'

Lynn made a point of shaking my hand, and held on to it for so long that Penny started to bristle. I retrieved my hand with something just short of brute strength, and Lynn smiled again as though she'd proved something.

'It's my job to help people through times of spiritual disturbance,' she said calmly. 'Can't you just feel the atmosphere? It's like the whole house is trying to speak to me, and we haven't even gone inside yet. We are definitely not alone here.'

I glanced quickly around at the rest of the group. None of them looked as if they were buying anything Lynn was selling, but they didn't say anything to challenge her. Perhaps someone had given them the speech about playing nicely with others. And Lynn was a celebrity, after all. She turned to Penny, considered her for a moment and then frowned dramatically.

'Oh, my dear . . . I sense an old horror hovering over you, weighing down on your life. You've suffered a loss in your family, haven't you?'

'Hasn't everyone?' said Penny, entirely unmoved.

Lynn turned back to me, still frowning hard to show us all how much she was concentrating. 'And you . . . have travelled a very long way to be here.'

'Could you be any more vague?' I said.

She grinned suddenly. 'If you like.'

The man standing behind Lynn decided he'd had enough of her performance and shouldered past her to thrust out a hand to me.

'Tom Shaw. Ghost-hunter. Part-time, of course. I've spent years searching for hard evidence of genuine afterlife phenomena. If there's anything going on here that shouldn't be, I have the technology to search it out and record it. When it comes to the weird stuff, science is our friend.'

A medium-height, middle-aged man, with a waistline he wasn't even trying to control any more, Tom was wearing a good suit that looked as though it didn't get out much. He had a square face, a stubborn look, and he was almost entirely bald. He shook my hand hard, to make it clear which one of us was in charge, and seemed a little surprised when I didn't even blink. He took his hand back, not even bothering to offer it to Penny, and fixed both of us with an accusing glare.

'It's about time the two of you got here. We've been standing around here for ages. I was assured we'd be inside Harrow House by eight o'clock sharp.'

'Life is full of little disappointments,' I said calmly.

Penny moved in quickly. 'Nice to meet you, Tom. I'm afraid our taxi ride took longer than we expected.'

'You were lucky to find someone prepared to bring you here,' said Lynn. 'All the drivers at the railway station turned us down, once we told them where we wanted to go. Some were quite rude about it.'

'I had to raise my voice to them,' said Tom.

'They really appreciated that,' said Lynn.

'In the end, my newspaper's connections got us a ride,' Arthur said smugly. 'I had my editor phone the owner of the local taxi firm and remind him just how much business we put his way, through advertising and mentions in our stories. One hand always washes the other in local papers.'

'We still had to crowd into the back of one taxi,' said Lynn. 'People around here have no idea how to treat a celebrity.'

'Pretending to put people in touch with their dead relatives in the back rooms of church halls does not make you a celebrity,' said Arthur. 'You only get your face in the paper because you're photogenic.'

'Well,' said Lynn. 'At least no one's ever going to accuse you of that.'

Arthur looked very much as if he wanted to say something, but Tom was already speaking again.

'We finally had to settle for a taxi whose driver had half a dozen crucifixes hanging off his steering wheel, and every window plastered with dangling chicken feet and voodoo charms.'

'You can never have too many protections,' Lynn said firmly. 'Especially when you're not sure what it is you're protecting yourself from.'

'He made me store my cases in the boot,' said Tom, with the air of someone still harbouring a grudge. 'I don't like being separated from my equipment.'

He gestured at two large suitcases, leaning against his legs like faithful dogs.

'What do you have in them?' I asked politely.

'Useful items,' said Tom, not giving an inch. 'It's important to have accurate readings in cases like this. Sometimes it's the smallest changes in your environment that can turn out to be the most significant. And there's nothing like a good early warning system to help you feel more secure.'

'But have you actually seen a ghost on any of your cases?' said Penny. 'Or recorded any evidence of one?'

'Not yet,' said Tom, just a bit defensively. 'It's all about being in the right place at the right time. With the proper equipment.'

'You can't rely on technology when it comes to the mysteries of the hidden world,' Lynn said serenely. 'You'll always need someone like me to provide spiritual help, for when science fails you.'

Rather than take part in an argument I just knew wasn't going anywhere helpful, I turned to the final member of Team Ghost, who'd been watching all of this and grinning broadly.

'Winifred Stratton!' she said loudly, before I could say anything. 'Call me Freddie! Everyone does!'

She strode past Tom so forcefully he actually fell back a step, displaced as much by the sheer force of her personality as anything else. Or perhaps he was just worried he'd get trampled underfoot. Freddie was a large and cheerful presence, a statuesque middle-aged woman with a handsome face and greying hair scraped back in a bun. She wore a shapeless tweed suit and a chequered waistcoat with food stains down the front. She seized my hand and pumped it hard.

'Good to meet you, Ishmael! I do love a good literary name. So – ready for the fray, are we?'

'Of course,' I said. 'Can't wait to get stuck in.'

'Good man! That's the spirit!' She flashed me a wide smile, dropped my hand as though she'd lost interest in it and turned to Penny, who already had both hands safely tucked behind her back.

'Are you really a white witch?' she asked politely.

'Oh, yes!' Freddie said happily. 'Got a diploma and everything. Bought it off the internet. Been checking up on me, have you?'

'We like to know who we're working with,' I said. 'I

understand you're also a local historian. How does that tie in with the spook-chasing?'

'Once you start digging into local events, you can't help but uncover all kinds of interesting stuff,' said Freddie, crossing her arms over her large bosom. 'The kind of things My Little Goth here likes to call the hidden world. I've been fascinated by the strange and uncanny ever since I was a nipper. And once I started reading the original sources, I became intrigued with the kind of weird happenings that never make it into the official records. What dear old Charles Fort used to call damned data: all the inconvenient and contrary facts that have to be ignored by established historians, because they raise far too many questions that can't be answered.'

'But what does that have to do with being a white witch?' said Penny.

'Fight fire with fire – that's what I say,' Freddie said cheerfully. 'When science can't protect you, and logic is off in a corner having a panic attack, magic is right there kicking arse and taking names. It's a much bigger world than most people realize, and magic can be very handy when it comes to making sense of things that would otherwise defy human comprehension.'

'But have you ever encountered anything unusual yourself?' I said.

'I've seen a few things,' said Freddie.

Something about the matter-of-fact way she said that impressed everyone. Apart from Arthur, who just scowled even more heavily.

'I don't believe in any of that stuff.'

'Then why are you here?' said Tom.

'Because I wasn't given any choice,' said Arthur.

He shoved his hands deep in his pockets, trying to look stern and determined, and hide the fact that he was shivering from the cold because he hadn't given enough thought to what he should be wearing.

'I was told you insisted on being here,' I said. 'In fact, that your being included in the investigation was a condition imposed by your family, so they'd have someone on hand to represent their interests.'

'Hah!' said Arthur loudly and bitterly. 'I'm only here because my editor insisted. He wants the inside story on how a group of local celebrity ghost-botherers spent the night in the most haunted house in Bath. Our readers eat that kind of thing up with spoons. And my family went along because all they care about is finally selling this dump. It's been hanging around the family's neck like a millstone for generations.'

'Bit of a big millstone,' I said.

'You have no idea,' said Arthur. 'I've had to put up with this crap ever since I was a kid. Once anyone finds out I'm part of the family that owns the notorious Harrow House, that's all they ever want to talk about. Ghosts . . . Hah! Give me a break.'

'Have you ever been out here before?' said Penny.

Arthur looked at her as though she was mad. 'Of course not.'

'Weren't you even curious?' I said.

'I am a reporter,' said Arthur, with as much dignity as he could manage. 'I deal in facts, not fairy stories.'

'So . . . you're not feeling any atmosphere of dread and horror right now?' Penny said carefully.

'No,' said Arthur emphatically.

'Then why do you have goose-bumps?' I said.

'Because it's cold!' Arthur looked very much as though he wanted to stamp his foot, but settled for glaring at everyone impartially. 'This is all just a waste of my time!'

'Then open the door and we'll get started,' I said. 'You do have the keys, don't you?'

'Of course,' said Arthur.

Tom gave him a hard look. 'You've had the keys all this time, while we've been standing around in the cold?'

'I was given strict instructions to wait outside until these two turned up,' said Arthur. 'Apparently, they have influence. Which is something else I'd like to know about . . .'

'Open the door,' I said.

He sniffed loudly, fumbled a ring of heavy metal keys out of his back pocket and used the largest to open the front door. The lock mechanism turned freely, but when Arthur tried to throw the door open dramatically, it wouldn't budge. He had to throw his whole weight against the door just to get it moving. The hinges didn't make a sound when the door finally swung back, and just as Dennis had described in the taxi, there was nothing beyond the door but darkness. A gloom so complete that even my more-than-human eyes couldn't make anything out. The door finally eased to a halt, but none of us made any move to enter Harrow House.

'There's something particularly disturbing about a darkness without even the slightest trace of light in it,' Lynn said quietly. 'It makes me think of being buried, or at the bottom of the ocean where the light cannot reach, or trapped in a night that goes on for ever because the sun never comes up.'

'Save the spooky chat for your clients,' said Arthur. 'Of course it's dark in there; I haven't turned the lights on yet.'

But for all his brave words, he still didn't move from where he was. Freddie produced a torch and sent its narrow beam flashing down the hallway. The light didn't travel far, but just its presence was enough to take away the dark's power.

'Always come prepared, as the actress should have said to the bishop,' Freddie said cheerfully.

I stepped into the hall, and Penny was quickly there beside me. Freddie moved in on my other side, flashing her torch's beam back and forth. Tom, Lynn and Arthur took their time bringing up the rear. The sound of our footsteps on the bare wooden floorboards seemed strangely flat, as though the sound itself was being suppressed by the sheer weight of the atmosphere.

'Hah!' Arthur said loudly. 'Let there be light!'

There was a sudden blaze of cold cheerless light from a chandelier halfway down the hall. Some of the bulbs didn't seem to be working, but there were enough to illuminate most of the long hallway. Freddie turned off her torch.

Arthur moved away from the light switch by the door, rubbing his hands together briskly. 'I was told there would be light, but no heat. No one's tried to fire up the ancient boiler in ages. And none of the windows have been opened for even longer than that, so expect things to be a bit on the stuffy side.' He smiled briefly. 'You're not seeing the house at its best, but then no one ever does.'

The oppressive atmosphere was stronger now we were inside: a definite feeling of dread, and horror, and fear of the unknown. None of which usually bothered me, but to my surprise I found I was having to fight down an urge to just turn around and leave. As though some inner voice was yelling at me to get out while I still could.

Without saying anything, Penny slipped her hand into mine. I held on to it tightly.

The air in the hallway was cold and still, and it smelled bad. Of damp and dust, and a definite suggestion of old things that hadn't been disturbed in far too long. I looked around at Team Ghost. They were all wrinkling their noses and shifting their feet unhappily, and I couldn't help noticing that we'd all come to a halt just a few feet inside the door.

There wasn't much to see in the hall. A few pieces of furniture, under covers thick with accumulated dust. Paintings lined both walls – the usual idyllic country views and hunting scenes. And a set of bare wooden stairs, leading up to the next floor. Nothing worrying, let alone threatening; nothing at all to justify what we were feeling. I gestured at the bare floorboards stretching away before us.

'Look at the thick layer of dust on the floor,' I said steadily. 'No one has walked down this hall in a very long time.'

'No one living,' said Lynn.

'That's the spirit!' Freddie said cheerfully. Tom gave her a pained look.

'I was told there were caretakers who came in here on a regular basis?' said Penny.

'So was I,' said Arthur. He sounded a little subdued. 'But it's as if no one's been in here for years.'

'Come on!' Tom said sharply. 'Let's get this show on the road, and let the dog see the rabbit. Before we all spook ourselves into nervous breakdowns.'

He opened one of the suitcases he'd brought in with him and sorted quickly through a variety of scientific instruments. Most of which looked as if they'd been cobbled together by someone who wasn't entirely sure what he was doing.

'Are you planning to measure the ghosts here?' I said politely.

'Everything in the world can be measured,' Tom said firmly,

not looking round from what he was doing. 'And if it can be
measured, it can be understood. That's what science does.'

'Not everything can be understood,' said Lynn. 'The world
is full of forces and mysteries beyond human comprehension.'

Tom ignored her, refusing to rise to the bait. He straightened
up, pointed some kind of scanner down the hallway and then
ostentatiously studied the resulting reading.

'What are you doing?' said Penny, just to show she was
taking an interest.

'Checking for heat sources,' said Tom. 'I'm not picking up
anything from anywhere in this house, apart from us . . .' He
looked round at the group. 'It's important to establish the background situation as soon as possible, so I can look for what stands
out. And I do like to make sure that there aren't any people in
the vicinity who shouldn't be here. There are some dubious types
who like to fake phenomena, for all kinds of reasons.'

'Yes,' said Arthur, not looking at anyone in particular, 'there
are, aren't there?'

'Those aren't standard cameras,' I said, peering into the
open suitcase.

'Well spotted,' said Tom, smiling for the first time. 'I
believe in covering all the bases, so I have wall cameras for
surveillance, including infrared and ultraviolet, along with
microphones that can pick up sounds well beyond the range
of the human ear. I've even got a few ex-military motion-
trackers, though don't ask me where I got them.'

Arthur looked as if he really wanted to, but a quick glance
round the group persuaded him this wasn't the moment.

'You can buy all kinds of ghost-hunting gear on line,' Tom
said expansively. 'But most of it is far too specialized for its own
good. Too much information just gets in the way, distracting you
from what really matters.' He tapped the side of his head solemnly.
'Eyes and ears, people; keep them open.'

Lynn decided that Tom had hogged the spotlight long enough.
She stepped away from the group and struck a dramatic pose.

'Human senses can be far more sensitive than anything
science can come up with,' she said grandly. 'We are all of
us surrounded by images from the past, by layers of history
stretching back into uncounted Time. All we have to do is open

ourselves to them. There are always voices calling out to us
for help, from lost souls unable to rest, if only we would listen.'
And then she broke off suddenly and looked sharply about her.
'What was that?'

'What was what?' I said politely.

'I heard something.' Lynn frowned, and I thought she seemed
honestly surprised, but she quickly resumed her professional
air. 'Something in this house just reached out to me . . . But
it wasn't like anything I've ever encountered before.'

'What did it sound like?' said Penny.

'Like someone calling my name . . .' Lynn shrugged, almost
angrily. 'I don't know.'

Tom produced a second scanner from his suitcase, fiddled
quickly with the settings and then turned it on Lynn, before
pointing it at the end of the hall.

'I'm not picking up anything,' he said flatly. 'All readings
are in the green, all systems are nominal. Nothing out of the
ordinary.'

'Something's here,' said Lynn. And something in her voice
held all of us where we were.

'Look,' said Tom. 'We can't just hang around here; we
need to choose a base of operations, so I can arrange for full
surveillance coverage.'

'And preferably somewhere with enough room for me to
lay down some heavy-duty protections,' said Freddie. 'Walking
into a haunted house without them is like skinny-dipping in
a pool packed with rabid alligators.'

'Do alligators get rabies?' said Arthur.

'You want to find out the hard way?' said Freddie.

Lynn was rubbing at her forehead with both hands, as
though troubled by a sudden headache or new and disturbing
thoughts. She glared down the hallway, concentrating hard,
listening for something the rest of us couldn't hear.

'This house is so full of old emotions it's broadcasting
like a radio station,' she said finally. 'I'm getting death, and
suffering, and a sense of things lost; old memories, rising up
out of deep Time . . .'

'You sound like a wine critic,' said Penny.

Everyone managed some kind of smile. Except for Lynn,

who looked around at Team Ghost and realized she'd lost her audience. She shrugged tiredly.

'Believe me or not,' she said. 'It doesn't matter. You'll see. Bad things happened here, and I think some of them are still happening.'

'Nothing supernatural has ever happened in this house,' I said firmly. 'The official reports were very clear.'

'It's the things that don't make it into official records that can do the most damage,' said Freddie.

'What kind of things?' said Penny.

Freddie didn't answer for a moment. She was too busy peering around and checking out the shadows to make sure they weren't getting up to anything she wouldn't approve of. She seemed to have lost some of her exuberance. As though the infamous Harrow House wasn't what she'd expected.

'It nearly always comes down to family secrets,' she said finally. 'Everything from incest to infanticide, and all kinds of physical and emotional abuse. You'd be surprised what people got away with, back in Victorian times. It was only a crime if it got reported.' She broke off, cocking her head on one side. 'What was that? Did any of you hear that?'

We all looked at each other and then listened hard. The hallway was so quiet I could hear everyone breathing, but nothing else.

'What did you hear?' said Lynn.

'A voice,' Freddie said slowly. 'But I couldn't understand anything it was saying.'

'Wonderful,' said Arthur. 'Only in the house five minutes and already you're hearing voices. Come on, people! Buildings like this are always going to be full of odd noises. It's just . . . the structure settling. Our entry into the hall probably changed the balance, or something.'

He went striding off down the hallway to make it clear the house wasn't getting to him, and then stopped and looked back when he realized no one else was going with him.

'This is just an empty old house!' he said loudly. 'Whoever buys this antiquated shit-hole should just tear it down and replace it with something modern. And comfortable. That would put an end to all the stories.' He stopped abruptly and shuddered. 'Damn, it's getting draughty in here. Will someone please shut the front door?'

We looked back and found the front door was already closed. Everyone stood very still.

'Who was the last person in?' said Tom.

'That would be me,' Arthur said slowly. 'And I didn't shut it. So who did?'

There was a general shaking of heads.

'Maybe it's specially weighted to close itself,' I said.

There was a lot of relieved nodding as Team Ghost decided they liked the sound of that.

'But then where did the draft come from?' said Penny.

To my surprise, Arthur actually looked pleased that something was happening. He started searching through his pockets.

'This is more like it! Strange happenings, with reasonable explanations. Maybe there is a story here, after all.'

He looked searchingly at everyone, checking their responses to the situation, like any good reporter. Lynn was frowning, lost in her own thoughts. She didn't seem at all happy that things were happening in Harrow House without asking her permission. Tom was checking one set of readings after another and shaking his head, as though his scanners were insisting on telling him things he didn't want to hear. Freddie had got her enthusiasm back and was looking eagerly in every direction, ready to go charging off and check out every shadowed nook and cranny – and then poke them with a stick to see what would happen.

I hadn't heard any voice or seen anything out of the ordinary. And I still thought the unpleasant atmosphere was most probably being generated by our own minds. Penny looked ready to take her cue from me, so I smiled reassuringly at her and she smiled back.

Arthur produced a small recording device from his back pocket, turned it on and thrust it into my face.

'You said the potential buyer of this house had security connections, Mr Jones. What did you mean by that?'

'I never said any such thing,' I said calmly. 'And neither should you. Now get that thing away from me. I don't do interviews.'

'He really doesn't,' said Penny.

'And why is that?' said Arthur, scowling at me challengingly.

'Because I have this regrettable tendency to take recording devices away from annoying reporters and stick them up their . . .'

'All right!' said Arthur. 'No need to get unpleasant!'

And then he stopped and scowled unhappily at his device. He shook it hard and slapped it a few times.

'What's wrong?' Penny said sweetly.

'The little light isn't on,' said Arthur. 'Which I think means the damn thing isn't working.'

Tom immediately hurried over, irresistibly drawn to any problem with technology. He took the device away from Arthur and studied it quickly.

'I can't see anything obviously wrong . . . Did you remember to check the batteries before you set out?'

'Of course I did!' said Arthur. 'For a reporter, that's like an actor checking his flies before he goes on stage.'

Tom shrugged and handed the device back to him. 'Maybe you should just take notes instead.'

'Excellent idea!' boomed Freddie. 'Don't worry, Arthur; I can teach you shorthand. And probably a few other things, too.'

She winked at him roguishly, and he stared back at her.

'That is sexual harassment.'

'Only if you do it right,' said Freddie.

Arthur started to smile and then remembered he was in a bad mood. He put the device back in his pocket.

'It could be the house,' said Lynn.

We all stopped and looked at her.

'What could be the house?' said Tom.

'Something in this place could be interfering with all of your devices,' said Lynn. 'The dead sometimes don't take kindly to being eavesdropped on. Which is ironic, if you think about it. We need to talk to this house. Make it clear we come in peace, and that we're ready to show proper respect for whatever may be here.'

'Oh, please!' said Arthur.

'Can we get a move on?' Freddie said loudly. 'It took me a long time to get permission to enter the legendary Harrow

House, and since we only have the one night to solve a mystery that goes back centuries, I don't feel like wasting time. So either the rest of you get the lead out of your socks or I'm off. If there are things here to be seen and heard, I want to see and hear them.'

'Aren't you even a little bit scared?' said Penny. 'Isn't the atmosphere getting to you at all?'

'Oh, yes,' Freddie said easily. 'But you can't let things like that bother you. Most haunted settings have a tendency to reflect back whatever emotions you bring in with you. Which is why your best defence in situations like this is a positive attitude. Try to see ghosts as just friends you haven't met yet.'

'What if they're not interested in being friends?' said Arthur.

Freddie grinned at him. 'Then let a smile be your armour. Because ghosts can stand anything except being laughed at.'

'You really don't give a damn, do you?' Arthur said admiringly.

'You have to go after what you want in this world,' said Freddie. She shot him a sly look. 'What do you want out of life, Arthur? Maybe I could help you get it.'

Arthur actually blushed. Freddie's grin broadened as she turned away to face Tom.

'Come on; pack up your toys and we'll go set up a base of operations. Let's get this investigation started!'

'Suits me,' said Tom. He dropped the scanners back into his case and snapped it shut with a flourish. 'Listen up, people; once we've found somewhere suitable, no one is to go wandering off on their own. I don't want my readings confused by unauthorized input.'

'But isn't that what an investigation is?' said Arthur, just to show he'd recovered his self-composure. 'Going everywhere and checking everything, to make sure it is what you think it is?'

'Science works best when you control all the variables,' said Tom.

'Boring!' Freddie said loudly.

'What do you think is in this house?' Penny quickly asked Freddie.

'Haven't the faintest,' she said cheerfully. 'I've read all the books on Harrow House, most of which are no better than they should be, and worked my way through most of the original reports in the local press . . . But none of them can agree on what's wrong with this place. Of course, Bath is no stranger to the weird stuff – everything from ghosts to the Beast of Brassknocker Hill and UFOs.'

'Really?' I said.

'There was a time, back in the seventies, when you couldn't look up at the sky without something looking back at you,' Freddie said solemnly. 'There was even some talk about a Somerset triangle. Of course, you can't believe everything you read in the papers.'

She dropped a wink to Arthur, and he actually smiled back at her.

'Don't blame the press for the kind of stories people want to read,' he said. 'There never was a local newspaper that wouldn't print something interesting but doubtful, rather than a dull fact. Reader beware . . .' He stopped abruptly and peered around him. 'But we never had to make up anything about this place. There's never been any shortage of stories when it comes to Harrow House. Some of them so disturbing no one would want to read them.'

'Like what?' Freddie said immediately, but Arthur just shook his head.

'I thought you were convinced this house's reputation was down to nothing more than old-time gossip and local scare stories?' I said.

'I am, and it is,' Arthur said firmly, getting a grip on himself. 'If there's one thing every reporter knows, it's that people love to make up stories.'

'There are far too many accounts of strange and unnatural events in this house to be dismissed so lightly,' said Lynn.

'Exactly!' said Freddie. She fixed Arthur with a thoughtful look. 'I've been sending requests to your family for years, to be allowed a good rummage around this house, and they've always turned me down. Sometimes quite rudely. So I was knocked off my pins when the family lawyers contacted me yesterday and asked if I wanted to be part of this group. Do you know what changed your family's mind?'

'Money, probably,' said Arthur. 'My family would agree to

anything to get this unwanted inheritance off their hands and out of their lives.'

'I was only contacted yesterday, too,' said Lynn.

'Same here,' said Tom. 'Why the sudden rush to get to the bottom of Harrow House, after all this time?'

Arthur just shrugged, so they all turned to look at Penny and me.

'No good asking us,' I said calmly. 'We're just hired hands.'

'The more I hear, the more convinced I am that something is going on,' said Arthur, looking accusingly around him.

'Something is always going on,' I said. 'We need to concentrate on what's *really* going on in this house.'

'Either you all shift your arses or I'm leaving you behind!' said Freddie. 'No more warnings!'

'Have you ever encountered an actual ghost?' Penny said quickly.

'Oh, yes,' said Freddie. Once again, her manner was so matter-of-fact that no one felt like challenging her.

'Weren't you frightened?' said Penny.

'Not at all, dear!' said Freddie. 'Ghosts are just people. Be nice to them, and they'll be nice to you.'

'That isn't always the case,' Tom said sternly. 'Some spirits can be manifestations of rage or emotional trauma – like poltergeists. We all have demons inside us.'

'Some more than others,' said Lynn.

'Do you honestly believe this house is haunted?' I asked Freddie.

'No doubt in my mind,' she said briskly. 'The question is: what by? Hauntings can take many forms. Revenants are the most common, of course – the dead walking in a place where they were once happy, or because of unfinished business. Then there's visions of the past, where bits of history burst through into the present. And there's always the genius loci – the spirit of the place – when so many bad things happen in one setting that it takes on a personality of its own. That's when people can get hurt, because places don't have human limitations.'

'And yet you keep saying you want to go off on your own,' said Penny.

'Oh, I'm already protected, dear. I'm so loaded down with

charms and amulets and blessings that it's a wonder I don't rattle when I walk.' Freddie stared thoughtfully down the hall. 'Still, I have to admit that Harrow House does not feel like a good place to be walking around with your soul hanging out. There are those who say this house is hungry . . .'

'Your positive attitude is slipping,' said Tom.

'Blow it out your science,' said Freddie.

'Ghosts are just people,' said Lynn. She used her most professional voice, to make it clear she was offering an expert opinion. 'Some are good, some are bad, and, of course, some are always going to be seriously disturbed, just from what they've been through. Ghosts can be dangerous, because people can be dangerous.'

'Treat someone as an enemy, and that's how they'll act,' Freddie said briskly. 'You should always keep an open mind, dear.'

'Oh, I don't think so,' said Lynn. 'You never know what might walk in.'

We all looked at her, not sure how to respond.

'I've always thought of hauntings as being a lot like the weather,' Tom said finally. 'They do what they do, and don't give a damn about how it affects us. Sometimes the wisest choice of action is simply to get out of the way and shelter somewhere safe until it's all over.'

'This is just an old house,' said Arthur, speaking slowly and distinctly, as though to a group of particularly obtuse children. 'There are always stories about old houses. They don't mean anything.'

'A base of operations is starting to sound really good to me,' I said. 'Somewhere easy to defend, where we can keep an eye on everything.' I looked at Arthur. 'Is there any room you'd recommend?'

He shrugged sullenly. 'I don't know! How would I know? I've never been here before. And no one in my family ever wants to talk about Harrow House.'

'Then let's start opening some doors,' I said. 'And see where they lead.'

'Of course,' said Penny. 'What could possibly go wrong?'

THREE
Somebody Dies

I looked down the hallway, and the hallway looked right back at me, determined to give nothing away. There were only three doors: one on the left, one to the right and one at the far end. None of them looked particularly dangerous – or inviting. So just to be contrary, I turned away and looked at the wooden stairs leading up to the next floor.

'Maybe we should try up there first?'

'Not a good idea,' Arthur said quickly.

'We need to search this floor thoroughly, before we go exploring upstairs,' said Tom. 'And besides, if anything should go wrong, it'd be a lot easier to get to the front door from here than all the way up there.'

'Bad experience in the past?' Penny said sweetly.

Tom shrugged. 'Just saying . . .'

'Nowhere is safe in Harrow House,' Lynn said flatly. Her Goth makeup exaggerated her frown, making it seem almost sinister. 'But I can't say I'm sensing any immediate danger.'

'You would if you went upstairs,' said Arthur. 'The upper floor is definitely not safe, because most of the floorboards are rotten.'

'How can you be so sure?' said Penny. 'You told us you'd never been here before.'

'I haven't,' he said crushingly. 'But it did occur to me to visit the estate agents before I came here, so at least I'd have some idea of what I was getting into. They warned me about all kinds of things, most of which I took with a whole handful of salt, but the one thing they were certain about was the state of the upper floor. "Treacherous" was the word they kept coming back to. Apparently, all it would take is one foot in the wrong place, and you could end up back on the ground floor without having to use the stairs.'

'Isn't he marvellous?' said Freddie. 'Half the time you can't get a word out of him, but get him started and he's a proper little speech machine.'

She punched Arthur encouragingly on the shoulder, hard enough to make him wince, and then marched off down the hallway. Lynn and Tom hurried after her, determined not to be left out of anything. Arthur started after them, but I stopped him with a hand on his shoulder. He shrugged the hand off and glared at me coldly.

'What?'

'Lock the front door,' I said quietly.

'Why?'

'To make sure we won't be disturbed. The last thing we need is uninvited visitors complicating things.'

He nodded reluctantly, located his keys again and locked the door. Penny and I strolled off down the hall after the others, leaving Arthur to catch up when he was done.

'Do you think the top floor is dangerous?' Tom was saying to Freddie.

'Seems likely,' said Freddie. 'Why would Arthur lie?'

'You tell me,' said Tom. 'He's your special friend.'

'And young enough to be your son,' said Lynn, peering disapprovingly at Freddie. 'You're old enough to know better.'

Freddie snorted happily, entirely unmoved. 'I'm old enough to know a lot of things that I will be only too happy to teach him.'

'At least now we know something for certain about Harrow House,' Tom said quickly. 'I'm a great believer in accumulating facts. You never know when they might come in handy. Especially when you're in enemy territory.'

'You think we might be in danger here?' I said, as Penny and I joined the group.

'Haunted houses are like minefields,' said Tom. 'You can never tell what might set them off.'

'Facts won't help you here,' said Lynn. 'This is a place of spirits and mysteries, of dangers to the soul as well as the body.'

'Am I the only one who winces every time she opens her mouth?' said Arthur, finally catching up with the rest of us.

That was enough to start yet another doctrinal argument, so I strode off down the hall, leaving Team Ghost to work out its own pecking order. Penny stuck close beside me as I headed for the left-hand door. It was properly closed and seemed almost defiantly ordinary. I leaned in close and listened carefully. I couldn't hear anything on the other side of the door, so I pushed it open. There wasn't a single protest from its hinges.

'That's not right, Ishmael,' Penny said quietly. 'Nothing in this house should be in such good condition, not after it's been left empty for so many years. In fact, apart from all this dust, I'd have to say that everything looks to be in perfect shape.'

'Except for the upstairs floors.'

'We only have Arthur's word for that.'

'Feel free to go up and check,' I said. 'I'll be right here, waiting to catch you.'

'Funny man,' said Penny.

'I suppose it's always possible that people have been coming and going in Harrow House for some time, on the quiet,' I said. 'For reasons of their own.'

'What kind of reasons?' said Penny. 'Oh! You think there might be hidden treasure here, after all?'

I had to smile at her sudden enthusiasm. 'Possibly. But let's deal with one problem at a time.'

I braced myself and pushed the door all the way back, but it was just a large empty room. Light spilled in from the hallway, enough to allow me to make out some heavy furniture lurking under dust sheets, but no signs of life or death anywhere. The only point of interest was that the room didn't have a window. Penny squeezed in beside me, gripping my arm tightly as she strained her eyes against the gloom.

'I can't see a damned thing.'

'There's nothing to be seen,' I said. 'And you might as well get used to that. I don't think there's anything in this house but myths and memories.'

'How can you be so sure?'

'Because if there was anything happening in this house, I would have picked up something long before this. Now, do you think I might have my arm back, please, before you cut off the circulation?'

'If there does turn out to be something nasty lurking in the shadows, I will never let you forget it,' said Penny, relaxing her grip but not letting go.

'Fair enough.'

The others had stopped arguing long enough to realize what Penny and I were doing, and they hurried over to crowd in behind us, rather than be left out of anything. I reached in past the door, found the light switch and turned it on. Flat yellow light revealed the shrouded furniture, like squatting ghosts, and yet more undisturbed dust on the floorboards. I pointed this out to Penny, and she nodded quickly.

'So much for your theory of people secretly coming and going,' she said quietly.

'Unless that's what we're supposed to think,' I said. 'Maybe they always leave fresh dust behind, to cover their tracks.'

Penny looked at me. 'Does that sound even a little bit likely?'

I shrugged. 'It did sound better in my head. In my defence, we have encountered stranger things in our time.'

'This is true,' said Penny.

'What are you two muttering about?' said Arthur, pressing right up against my back so he could peer over my shoulder.

'Just agreeing that there's nowhere here anyone could be hiding,' I said. 'Though it does look like your caretakers have been sleeping on the job.'

I turned off the light and pulled the door shut, making sure it closed properly. I didn't want it suddenly swinging open again and freaking everyone out. I turned around and stared hard at Team Ghost until they got the message and fell back, and then I marched across the hall to the right-hand door. Penny followed close behind, but the others took their time, dragging their feet in the rear. Presumably on the grounds that if something bad was about to happen, they'd much rather it happened to someone else first.

I listened hard at the door, and once again I couldn't hear anything. I opened the door and turned on the light, revealing more sheeted furniture in another empty room. A grandfather clock stood off to one side, its hands frozen at three o'clock.

I wondered if that was when the original family had been forced out of their home, never to return.

'More dust on the floor . . . but I'm not seeing any cobwebs, Ishmael,' Penny said thoughtfully. 'In fact, I don't think I've seen a single cobweb anywhere. Have you?'

'No.' I said. 'That is a bit odd. Perhaps Harrow House's reputation is so bad that no self-respecting spider would want to come here.'

The others arrived and crowded in behind us, breathing down our necks and craning their heads for a better view.

'Could be a parlour, I suppose,' said Arthur. 'Or a drawing room, or even a library . . .'

'That's not a library, dear,' said Freddie.

'How can you be so sure?' said Arthur.

'No bookshelves and no books.'

'And no window,' said Penny. 'Just like the other room.'

'Doesn't exactly look cheerful, whatever it is,' said Tom. 'This is starting to feel less like touring a stately home and more like excavating a tomb.'

'No,' said Freddie. 'I've done that. And it was a lot more fun than this.'

'Did you find a mummy?' said Lynn.

'No,' said Freddie. 'She was out.'

She snorted loudly at her own joke. No one else felt like joining in.

'Are any of you still feeling the oppressive atmosphere?' Penny said suddenly. 'Only . . . I'm not.'

Team Ghost took a moment to think about that, and going by the sudden surprise on their faces, none of them had noticed when the bad mood dropped away. I had; it lost its hold on me the moment I started down the hall to check out the doors.

'Told you it was all in our minds,' said Arthur.

A thought struck me, and I turned to look at him. 'Given that this house was abandoned back in Victorian times, and no one has lived here since, when was the electricity put in?'

Arthur shrugged, which I was beginning to think was his default response to any question.

'Probably just another doomed attempt to make the house

seem more attractive to potential buyers. Back when my family still had some hope of shifting the burden to someone else. God knows they've tried enough enticements down the years, including prices so low they bordered on bribery, and sending emotionally blackmailing letters to all kinds of historical societies. Maybe they should try "Buy one, get one free!" or "Do you like feeling severely depressed, and enjoy throwing your money away? Then have we got a house for you!"'

'Hasn't anyone lived here, since your ancestors left?' said Penny.

'Not since they ran screaming out into the night, on the fourteenth of September 1889,' said Arthur. 'We can be sure of the exact date, because they made so much noise that all the neighbours came running out to see what was happening. It was covered by all the local papers. I've read the original stories, in the *Herald*'s archives. My ancestors said things had got so bad here that they were literally driven out, but not by any actual apparition or strange noises, or any of the usual horror shows . . . It was more like the house just didn't want them around any more. But don't ask me what actually happened, back on that fateful night, because I don't have a clue.'

'Because your family doesn't like to talk about it,' said Penny.

'Got it in one,' said Arthur. 'Not then, and not now. There was a hell of a lot of speculation in the press at the time, and even more local gossip – most of it pretty unsavoury – but all anyone knows for certain is that the head of the family, a very successful businessman called Malcolm Welles, took his wife and children and left the country, never to return.'

'Someone must have tried to live here after that,' I said.

Arthur scowled angrily. 'I wish you'd stop treating me like I'm some kind of expert! All I know for sure is that while all kinds of people have tried to live here, down the years, not one them even lasted till morning.'

'And yet none of them ever reported seeing a ghost?' I said.

Arthur shrugged. 'So they say.'

'And you still don't believe there's anything unusual going on here?' said Penny.

Arthur glared around him defiantly. 'Give a house a bad enough name, and people will do the rest for themselves.'

'If Harrow House has such a bad reputation,' I said, 'and no one wants it at any price, why do the estate agents still have it on the market?'

'Because my family insists,' said Arthur. 'I think they're hoping that someday they'll find a buyer who's deaf and blind to the atmosphere, and immune to hauntings. Though that hasn't worked out too well so far.'

'Why has no one ever tried to break in and squat?' said Freddie. 'Homeless people must have more pressing things to worry about than ghosties and ghoulies. And why hasn't the house been vandalized, or even burned down, if the locals hate it so much?'

'No one has ever tried to squat here,' Arthur said flatly. 'You can draw your own conclusions as to why. And none of the children round here dare get close enough to even throw stones at the windows.'

I remembered the taxi driver's story, but said nothing.

'I've no doubt there are any number of local residents who would be only too happy to burn the house down, if they could do it from a safe enough distance,' said Arthur, warming to his theme. 'If only for their own peace of mind. But the general feeling seems to be that they don't want to upset whatever's in here. Or risk doing anything that might let it loose.'

Lynn shook her head. 'And yet you still insist . . .'

'Yes, I do still insist!' Arthur said loudly. 'All right, I might have felt . . . something, when I came in, but I'm fine now. This is just an old house, and the rest is just stories! I'm a reporter; I know all about the stories people make up, to make themselves feel like they're a part of something important.'

He looked challengingly round the group.

'It was a bad feeling,' Freddie said finally. 'But I've felt worse.'

'Same here,' said Tom.

We all looked at Lynn, but our resident psychic just stared calmly back at us, saying nothing.

'You're supposed to be our spiritual advocate,' I said. 'What are you feeling right now, Lynn? Anything?'

'We're not alone in this house,' Lynn said carefully. 'I'm getting a definite feeling of being watched, but I can't say by what. I'm not picking up any sense of an occupying spirit. No surviving personality, no lingering presence from the past . . . Whatever is in this house with us, it's like nothing I've ever encountered before. The best way I can put it . . . is that it feels like this house is in a really bad mood.' She stopped and smiled briefly. 'Of course, I could be wrong.'

Penny caught my eye, and we moved away from Team Ghost as they tried to press Lynn to be more specific.

'Ishmael . . . how are we supposed to prove a house isn't haunted?' Penny said quietly. 'The buyer isn't going to be satisfied with some vague account of a spooky atmosphere that didn't last. Can we present a lack of evidence as evidence?'

'There have never been any sightings of actual ghosts in this house, or any paranormal experiences as such,' I said carefully. 'What we felt could have been nothing more than everyone reinforcing each other's mood. So I suppose we take a good look round, stay here till the morning and see what happens.'

'What if nothing happens?'

'Then that's what we report.'

'Hey!' Arthur said sharply. 'No secrets! What are the two of you muttering about now?'

'Just debating whether either of these rooms would serve as a base of operations,' I said easily.

Tom shook his head. 'I'd prefer more space, if possible, to allow proper coverage by my surveillance equipment.'

'There's one more door, at the end of the hall,' I said. 'Though I feel I should point out that if that room turns out to be unsuitable as well, we'll have to drag some chairs out into the hall and set up camp here.'

'No,' Tom said immediately. 'We'd be too open to attack in the hall.'

'Attack?' said Penny. 'From what?'

'Isn't that what we're here to find out?' said Lynn.

'I should have brought my old hockey stick,' said Freddie.

She smiled wistfully. 'I used to be a real devil on the playing field, back in my plucky youth.'

I went back to turn off the room's light and shut the door firmly, and then I set off down the hall with Penny striding it out beside me. Team Ghost hurried after us. They seemed to be feeling a bit braver now that nothing bad had happened in either of the other rooms. I walked right up to the final door, opened it with a flourish and threw it back with enough force that the door slammed hard against the inside wall. The noise made everyone else jump, just a bit. I turned on the light and then stepped back so everyone could take a look.

It was definitely the biggest of the three rooms, with yet more furniture under dust sheets, including what appeared to be a grand piano. Half a dozen paintings hung on the walls, depicting yet more rustic scenes. Most of them looked as if they could use a good clean. A rather striking portrait hung over the empty fireplace . . . and finally there was a single window, hidden away behind closed curtains. The floor had the usual layer of undisturbed dust. I allowed the others enough time for a good look round and then strolled into the room, with Penny beside me. Team Ghost clustered together outside the door, content to watch and see how we got on.

I wandered round the room, taking my time. Once I was sure nothing was going to leap out and attack me, I came to a halt before the large portrait above the fireplace. A formidable Victorian patriarch stared back at me with piercing eyes, a grim mouth and massive muttonchop whiskers. Either he really hadn't enjoyed sitting for his portrait or the painter had perfectly captured his subject's constant bad mood. He certainly had the look of a man prosperous enough that he didn't normally have to put up with anything he didn't want to.

Tom was the first to follow us in. He dropped his suitcases on the floor and nodded quickly.

'This will do. Only the one entrance to defend, and enough space to get good coverage and clear readings. I can work here.'

'I'm so glad you approve,' said Arthur, slouching in after him.

He took in what Penny and I were looking at, and came over to scowl at the portrait.

'That is the man himself: Malcolm Welles. A cut-throat businessman – *literally*, some said, when he was first starting out – and extremely successful. He was something to do with transportation . . . canals to begin with, and then the railways. But don't ask me what he transported. It must have been extremely profitable; Malcolm Welles was famously the richest man in Bath, at a time when that took some doing. He's supposed to have designed this house personally.'

'I can't see that any of it did him a lot of good in the long run,' said Penny.

'Can't argue with that,' said Arthur. 'Handsome devil, isn't he?'

'Not really,' said Penny.

Arthur shrugged. 'He was rich. Rich trumps handsome.'

By now Freddie was marching around the room, studying everything with a keen interest, while Lynn had taken up a position in the middle of the room. She stood very still, frowning thoughtfully, as though taking the room's spiritual temperature. Or perhaps just considering her options. Tom had opened both his suitcases and was rummaging cheerfully through their contents.

'Let's get these dust sheets off the chairs,' I said to Penny. 'So at least we'll have somewhere to sit.'

'There's a lot of them, for one room,' said Penny.

'Must be a sitting room,' I said.

She gave me a long-suffering look.

We set about removing the heavy sheets, raising huge clouds of dust that made everyone cough and sneeze. The chairs turned out to be large over-stuffed things with stiff backs – functional rather than comfortable.

Arthur threw himself into one and slumped bonelessly, scowling at everything. Lynn curled up in another, her tiny figure in the huge chair making her look like a child who'd overdone the scary makeup for Halloween. Penny went over to the window and looked at the closed curtains thoughtfully. I moved in beside her.

'This is the only window we've found so far,' she said. 'Could the others have been bricked up?'

'No,' I said. 'I checked. The only windows I saw outside were all upstairs.'

'But why design a house with only one window on the ground floor?'

'Maybe Malcolm Welles didn't want anyone looking in.'

'What was he afraid people might see?' said Penny.

'Perhaps whatever it was that drove him and his family out.'

Penny tried to open the curtains, but the heavy drapes didn't want to cooperate. I had to force them open with sheer brute strength, and that was when we discovered that the window had been nailed shut. With a hell of a lot of nails.

'Why would anyone want to do that?' said Penny.

'To keep something out,' I said. 'Or possibly in.'

I peered through the dusty glass, but all I could see was the endless dark of the night. I looked at it for a long moment.

'You're frowning, Ishmael,' said Penny. 'Why are you frowning, and should I be getting ready to run or hit something?'

'I should be able to see something out there,' I said slowly. 'I know the grounds are surrounded by high walls, but I can't even make out the moon or the stars.'

'Maybe it's an overcast night,' said Penny.

'Maybe,' I said.

I turned away to see what Team Ghost were getting up to. Lynn was still lost in her own thoughts. Arthur looked as though he wanted to start an argument but couldn't raise the energy. Tom was humming tunelessly as he assembled his scientific equipment. And Freddie was kneeling before a large wooden cabinet, its doors thrown wide open.

'Come and look at this!' she said loudly. 'Someone in this house was into taxidermy in a really big way.'

'Am I the only one thinking of the film *Psycho*?' Penny murmured.

We were the only ones interested enough to join Freddie and stare politely at a number of badly stuffed owls, foxes, cats and what I think was meant to be a squirrel. All of their stances were horribly unnatural, the shapes of the bodies were marred by unfortunate bulges, and the glass eyes glared madly.

'Amateur night,' Freddie said dismissively. 'Any self-respecting professional would have turned up his nose at results like these and started again. Probably in a whole new occupation.'

'It was probably somebody's hobby,' said Penny. 'They had to do something until television was invented. The Victorians were interested in all kinds of weird things.'

'I suppose it's always possible it's these animals' ghosts that are roaming the house,' said Freddie, levering herself to her feet. 'Seeking revenge for this affront to their dignity.'

I turned away to check out Tom, who was carefully positioning four of his wall cameras so he could be sure he had the whole room covered. He then bustled about setting up microphones and temperature gauges, along with a whole bunch of other stuff I didn't even recognize, before finally powering up a monitor screen that showed all four camera feeds simultaneously. Tom sat cross-legged before it, tapping quickly at his laptop's keyboard. Constantly changing readings appeared down one side of the screen.

'All the cameras are on line . . . We are now covered!' he said grandly.

'Good for you,' said Arthur, not stirring from his chair. 'Anyone want to do their party piece?'

'Nothing can happen in this room now, without us knowing,' Tom said firmly. 'My instruments are maintaining a constant watch on sight, sound, temperature . . . and atmospheric and electromagnetic conditions.'

'Whereas we only have eyes and ears,' said Arthur.

'They can't record,' said Tom, refusing to be put off by Arthur's lack of appreciation. 'The whole point of science is being able to prove that what you experienced actually happened.'

'You did say earlier that you'd never been able to record anything substantive,' said Penny.

'Good word,' I said.

'I thought so,' said Penny.

Tom shrugged, not taking his eyes off the screen. 'Things have a tendency to happen quickly in places like this. Paranormal phenomena can be very elusive, very hard to pin down.'

'So you're recording everything that's here?' said Penny.

'If it moves, I'll have a permanent record of it,' said Tom.

Penny caught my eye, and we moved away from the others.

'Are you worried about appearing in Tom's recordings?' she said quietly.

'Of course,' I said, just as quietly. 'The Organization goes to a lot of trouble to hide me from the world's surveillance systems, and with good reason. So I'll just have to make sure I wipe all of Tom's recordings before I leave here.'

'That's a bit hard on Tom, isn't it?'

'It would be harder on me, if any of them got out.'

And then we all looked round sharply as Lynn made a startled sound. She was sitting bolt upright in her chair, her eyes wide in the midst of all the mascara.

'What?' said Arthur, sitting up straight despite himself.

'Did you see something, Lynn?' said Tom, quickly turning his attention back to the readings scrolling down his screen.

'I heard something,' said Lynn. 'Though I doubt it was anything that would show up on your equipment. I keep telling you: we're not alone in this house. There is a definite presence here . . . And I don't think it's anything your science can protect us from.'

'I thought you said there weren't any ghosts here?' I said.

'Nothing I can recognize as a spirit,' said Lynn. 'And the very fact that I can't tell what it is disturbs the hell out of me.'

'Oh, give me a break,' said Arthur, settling back in his chair. 'Save the spooky performance for a paying audience.'

'What exactly did you hear, Lynn?' said Penny.

'I'm almost sure it was a voice,' Lynn said slowly. 'But I couldn't understand anything it was saying. And, Arthur, whatever's in this house was frightening enough to drive out an entire family in 1889 and make sure they never came back. Including a man who, from the look of his portrait, didn't scare easily.'

'Which is why I've been busy laying down some decent wards and protections,' said Freddie.

She pointed proudly back and forth at the strange markings she'd drawn all around the room, on the walls and on the floor. A whole bunch of weird symbols, in a variety of different coloured chalks.

'Interesting,' I said. 'Particularly because I don't recognize any of them – and I've been around.'

'It's true,' said Penny. 'He has.'

'My system is derived from a number of ancient magical traditions,' Freddie said cheerfully. 'Egyptian, Sumerian, Babylonian . . . Go with what's been proven to work – that's what I say. I wasn't given enough time to prepare properly, or I would have brought along some of the artefacts I've collected that can really punch their weight.'

'Why would we need them?' said Penny.

Freddie stopped smiling and looked round the room as though daring it to start something. 'Because I don't trust this house. It has secrets, and quite possibly an agenda of its own.'

'The instruments I've set up are perfectly capable of protecting us,' Tom said stubbornly.

'Science can't protect anyone from a spiritual attack,' said Lynn.

'To be fair, there are hardly any accounts of ghosts who want to harm the living,' said Freddie.

She was doing her best to sound confident, but it seemed to me that she was trying to convince herself as much as us. She frowned briefly, as though pushing away an unwanted thought, and pressed on.

'Malevolent ghosts are a modern idea, and mostly the fault of bad movies.'

'What about poltergeists?' said Penny. 'Or does that come under the heading of bad movies?'

'Oh, no,' Freddie said immediately. 'I liked that one. The original, of course, not the sequels. But poltergeists aren't anything to do with ghosts; they fall under the heading of weird phenomena produced by the living. Usually a troubled teenager. Remove them from the setting, often with a good boot up the backside, and the problems stop. Ghosts are different. It's important to remember that they're only people, doing their best to communicate with us.'

'Then why do they scare people so much?' said Penny.

Freddie shrugged. 'Because of what they represent.'

'A ghost is positive proof of the mind's survival after death,' Tom said firmly. 'That's why it's so important to get our understanding of these phenomena on a proper scientific footing. Think of the possibilities, if we could talk to those who have gone before us. The things they could tell us . . . What a comfort that could be.'

'Not necessarily,' said Lynn, and something in her voice turned all our attention back to her. She wasn't looking at all happy for someone who should have been in her element. 'It all depends on what happens once we've left this world. The afterlife may not be anything like what we've been led to believe. And considering some of the things spirits have communicated to me, I have to wonder if we're capable of understanding what happens after death. It may be that heaven and hell are just limited human concepts.'

No one had anything to say in response to that, so we all just sat in our chairs and waited for something to happen.

The room was very still. The only sounds I could hear came from people stirring restlessly. Tom stared unwaveringly at his screen. I kept a watchful eye on the door, and occasionally the window. Time passed.

'I'm starting to think this might be just a wild ghost chase,' Freddie said finally. 'If you ask me, Harrow House is rather letting the side down. I mean, no spirits, no moving objects, not even an oppressive atmosphere any more . . . This is not what I signed on for.'

'I can't even use my phone,' Arthur said glumly. 'The estate agents made a point of telling me that there's no signal up here. God, I'm bored . . .'

'Come and join me in my chair,' said Freddie. 'I'm sure we can think of something to do to outrage the spirits.'

Tom made a sudden surprised sound, and we all turned to look at him. He was leaning forward, staring intently at the changing readings on his screen.

'The temperature in this room just dropped four degrees,' he said sharply. 'Didn't any of you feel it?'

Tom looked quickly round the group, but all he got in return was baffled looks and shaking heads. He went back to concentrating on his readings, as we all got up out of our chairs and stared about us.

'The temperature seems to have stabilized,' Tom said slowly. 'But now I'm getting some really odd electromagnetic variations . . .'

'What does that mean?' said Arthur.

'I don't know,' said Tom. 'I've never seen anything like this.'

And then we all turned sharply to look at the door, as people started talking out in the hall. Loud strident voices, overlapping each other in one great meaningless babble. Whoever it was, they sounded as though they were right outside. Like a party we hadn't been invited to. We all stared at the closed door, but none of us moved to open it. I strained my ears, but I couldn't make out a single word I understood. And then the whole thing just stopped, as suddenly as it had begun. For a long moment there was nothing but silence. I turned to Tom.

'Were those real noises?'

'What do you mean, were they real? We all heard them!'

'But were you able to record them?' I said pointedly.

He checked quickly. 'No . . . I've got nothing! How is that even possible? We all heard them.'

I looked at the closed door.

'I really wouldn't,' Lynn said quickly. 'We have no idea what might be out there.'

'Exactly,' said Freddie. 'And we need to know.'

I headed for the door. Freddie came with me, and Penny quickly moved in on my other side. I pulled the door open; the hall was completely empty. I'd made a point of leaving the lights on, in case something happened, and I could see all the way down the hallway to the front door. There was no sign of life anywhere, nothing to suggest who or what might have been talking.

'Could someone else have got into the house?' said Freddie.

'I had Arthur lock the front door,' I said. 'Just to make sure we wouldn't be disturbed.'

She looked at me sharply. 'And you didn't think to tell us?'

'What difference would it have made?' I said reasonably. 'It's not like we're going anywhere until the morning comes.'

'It's the principle of the thing!' said Freddie.

'I don't have any principles,' I said.

'I am not going anywhere near that,' said Penny.

I closed the door carefully and moved back to join Tom. He was glaring at the readings on his screen, as though he could force them to change into something that made more sense.

'If there'd been anything out there, my motion-trackers should have kicked in and sounded an alarm,' he said tightly.

'What kind of range are we talking about?' said Penny.

'All of the ground floor, plus some of the stairs,' said Tom. 'And my trackers are supposed to be sharp enough to detect a mouse sticking its head out of its hole.'

'Could someone have got into the house before we did?' I said.

'My family has the only set of keys,' said Arthur.

'What about the estate agents?' said Freddie.

'They have to ask us for them,' said Arthur. 'On the increasingly rare occasions they agree to come out here with a prospective buyer.'

And then he stopped and quickly checked his back pocket to make sure his keys were still there. Reassured, he pressed on.

'And anyway, remember the thick dust on all the floors? No one could have got in without leaving a hell of a lot of footprints. We are the first people to have entered this house in a very long time and, no, I haven't forgotten about the damn caretakers. They must have been pocketing our money for years and doing damn all to earn it! You can bet I'll be having some serious words with my family about that, once this is over.'

He finally wound down and we all stood looking at each other. It was very quiet. Freddie beamed suddenly and rubbed her hands together.

'Well! At least something is finally happening!'

'Yes,' said Arthur. 'But what?'

'Voices,' said Lynn. 'Voices from the other side . . . Am I the only one who keeps seeing sudden movements out of the corner of my eye?'

We all looked quickly around us, but everything seemed normal, no matter how fast we turned our heads.

'Probably just floaters in your eyes,' said Tom. 'I should have them checked if I were you.'

'We're all getting a bit jumpy,' said Arthur, in what he probably thought of as his reasonable voice. 'This is all just standard haunted-house bullshit: making a big thing out of unexpected noises, seeing things that aren't really there.

I'm sure we'll find perfectly reasonable explanations for all of this.'

'Like what?' said Tom.

'How about stray radio signals being picked up and broadcast by your equipment?' said Arthur.

Tom started to say something and then didn't. Arthur nodded knowingly.

'You're all just spooking yourselves.'

'Sorry, dear,' said Freddie. 'But I'm not buying it. Harrow House is finally starting to live up to its reputation. We can't just sit around here; we need to be doing something! I say we search this house from top to bottom, and, yes, Arthur, that does include upstairs!'

'What if we poke our noses into everything and still nothing happens?' said Penny.

'Then we do whatever it takes to make something happen!' said Freddie.

'Going upstairs isn't safe,' Arthur said stubbornly. 'If one of us should crash through the floorboards and break a leg, it might be a really long time before we could persuade an ambulance to come all the way out here.'

'If we don't go looking for whatever is inhabiting this place,' Lynn said quietly, 'it will come looking for us. And not in a good way.'

Freddie looked at me challengingly. 'You're the reason we're here; what do you think we should do?'

'We came here to determine whether or not this house is haunted,' I said steadily. 'And I don't think it would go down very well if we were forced to admit tomorrow that we spent the whole night sitting in one room. I think we should at least explore a little.'

'Now you're talking!' said Freddie. 'Get out there and bang the drum, scare up some action!'

'But before anyone goes anywhere,' said Lynn, 'I think we need to hold a seance.'

We all looked at her, and she stared calmly back.

'Has it really come to that?' said Arthur.

'A seance is the best way to reach out to whatever is in

here with us,' Lynn said patiently. 'Harrow House has been trying to talk to us. It has something to say.'

'But is it something we want to hear?' said Penny.

I looked at her.

'I'm just joining in,' she said.

'We need to reassure the house that we're here to help,' Lynn said firmly. 'Try to find out what it needs to be at rest.'

Tom shook his head and gestured firmly at his instruments. 'This is how we'll make contact – in a controlled and scientific manner.'

'All you can do is watch and wait,' said Freddie. 'We need to be a damn sight more proactive!'

'You want to poke Harrow House with a stick?' I said. 'Just to see what happens?'

'We need to open a line of communication with the house, before we do anything else,' said Lynn.

'And say what?' said Arthur. '"Please stop bothering people"?'

'Lynn could have a point,' Freddie said reluctantly. 'Ghosts are only people. How would you like it if a bunch of strangers barged into your house and didn't even try to talk to you?'

'Do witches believe in seances?' said Penny.

'I don't *not* believe in them,' Freddie said carefully.

'Well, would you believe it,' said Arthur, patting his pockets ostentatiously. 'I didn't think to bring my Ouija board with me!'

'We don't need one,' said Lynn, not rising to the bait. 'All we have to do is sit in a circle and open ourselves to what's here.' She smiled suddenly. 'And it beats tiptoeing over rotten floorboards, doesn't it?'

We all managed some kind of nod. If only because Lynn was so determined, and none of us wanted to make a scene. Tom looked dubiously round the room.

'If we're really going to do this, it has to be properly recorded. I'll need to adjust the cameras and the microphones, to make sure everything that happens is covered.'

'Go ahead,' said Lynn, like a mother indulging a child with a new toy. 'It'll take me a while to prepare myself anyway.'

She picked a spot in the middle of the room, pushed a few chairs back out of the way, and then sat down and assumed a full lotus with an ease I could only admire. Her wicker bag had never left her shoulder during any of this, and she hugged it to her protectively as she gathered her thoughts. Tom banged away at his keyboard, and I heard soft whirring sounds from the wall cameras as they adjusted their focus. Freddie did a quick tour of the room, checking her symbols and reinforcing them if they looked a bit scuffed. Arthur wandered along with her. I concentrated my hearing on the two of them.

'Are you worried the seance might interfere with your protections?' Arthur said politely.

'Not really,' said Freddie. 'But it's always a good idea to make sure your safeguards are working, if you're going to open your mind in a dangerous place.'

'That sounds . . . creepy.'

'Oh, it can be,' said Freddie. 'Not everything in the spirit world is our friend. So, better safe and secure than really, really sorry.'

'But what are you protecting us from?' said Arthur.

'Whatever drove your family out of this house.'

'You said ghosts are just people . . .'

'People can get angry if you give them good enough reason,' said Freddie. 'So, tread softly and carry a big magical stick.'

Arthur smirked. 'Do you have it hidden about you?'

'Would you like to search me?'

They shared a smile.

'I'm glad I met you,' said Arthur.

'Right back at you, dear.'

Arthur looked at her steadily. 'You honestly think we're in danger here?'

Freddie draped a companionable arm across his shoulders. 'Don't worry; I won't let anything happen to you. Or, at least, nothing you don't want.'

Arthur grinned at her. 'Here's to you, Mrs Robinson.'

They laughed quietly together.

I turned to Penny and lowered my voice until only she could hear me. 'Once the seance starts, watch everyone. If one of them is planning something, that's when they'll do it, while the rest of us are preoccupied.'

'What do you think might happen?' said Penny.

'I think someone is going to try to sell us a bill of goods,' I said. 'Probably try to convince us they've made contact with something, so they can send us off chasing shadows, and they can get on with whatever they're really here for.'

'Do you think there really could be treasure hidden in this house?' said Penny, bouncing eagerly on her toes.

'Something is being hidden from us,' I said. 'And, Penny . . . keep a specially close eye on Lynn; I don't trust her. It's not like I trust any of them, but she strikes me as the one most likely to have a secret agenda.'

We both looked round as Lynn raised her voice, asking everyone to form a circle sitting on the floor. She spoke in a calm, practised voice, as though she did this sort of thing all the time and knew what she was doing. I think we were all a little impressed, but we still hesitated, standing around and looking at each other. Arthur turned to Freddie.

'Have you ever taken part in a seance before?'

'I've done a bit of everything, in my time,' Freddie said comfortably. 'My motto is: never put off till tomorrow what you can do today. Because if you do it today and you like it, you can do it again tomorrow.'

Penny looked at her. 'Do you expect this seance to do any good?'

'It's worth a try,' said Freddie. 'And as long as we all act sensibly, it shouldn't do any harm.'

'I don't know,' I said. 'I pity the poor ghost that makes contact with us.'

'Play nicely, Ishmael,' said Penny. She smiled determinedly at everyone. 'I'm afraid Ishmael doesn't believe in ghosts. I mean, *really* doesn't believe.'

Lynn bestowed her kindest and most indulgent smile on me. 'If half of what they say about Harrow House is true, it will make a believer out of you.'

'Not unless a ghost walks right up to me and spits in my eye,' I said firmly. I switched my gaze to Freddie. 'What do you think will happen if we do this?'

'Beats me,' she said cheerfully. 'My art is all about nature. I can whistle up a wind, or gentle a storm . . . Charm an angry soul, touch a cold heart or ease a troubled mind. But death and its dominions are way outside my chosen skill set.'

'If you're all about life, why are you so keen on chasing ghosts?' I said bluntly. 'The very definition of being not at all alive?'

'I'm here to solve the mystery of Harrow House,' said Freddie. 'I want to know what really happened here, all those years ago. I was a local historian long before I was a witch, and I've been researching this place for years. Because although everyone calls it a haunted house, it doesn't act like one. Harrow House is a mystery, wrapped in an enigma, nailed to a complete pain in the arse.'

'Then tell us, historian,' I said. 'What did happen here? Originally?'

Freddie turned courteously to Arthur. 'This is your family's house. You should be the one to tell the story.'

'But you're the local expert,' he said quickly. 'You're bound to know lots more than I do.'

Freddie beamed at all of us, happy for a chance to show off her expertise. We all listened carefully as she launched into her lecture – except for Lynn, who was still busy sitting on the floor, looking thoughtful.

'The one thing all the stories agree on,' Freddie said cheerfully, 'is that something bad happened in this house, long before the family ran screaming into the night in 1889. But no one knows what. It wasn't a murder, or a mysterious disappearance – nothing to attract attention to the family. Most historians believe it must have been connected with Malcolm Welles's business. He was not a well-liked man, and there are all kind of rumours about what he did to raise the money he needed to get his business started. There are even darker suggestions about exactly what it was that he transported. But whatever he did to bring about his sudden expulsion from this house, it was so bad it tainted the wood and stone of Harrow House forever. Which probably explains why we all felt the way we did when we walked through the front door.'

I looked politely at Arthur. 'Does that sound right to you?'

He shrugged. 'It fits with what I've heard. But as I keep saying, it's mostly just rumour and guesswork. No one knows anything for sure.'

'Don't you have any idea what it was your ancestor Malcolm did to make his fortune?' said Penny.

'Nobody knows,' Arthur said firmly. 'Before he left this country, Malcolm sold off all his business interests and burned his private papers. Which, of course, isn't at all suspicious. Ever since, my family has been damned by association. But nothing bad has happened in this house for over a century! That's a fact! And no one has ever been hurt here – just spooked!

'I keep telling my family, the best thing we could do is just give up and embrace the weird stuff. Use this nonsense as a selling point. Open up the house to tourists who are into that kind of thing, and treat it as one big ghost train. Prove to everyone it's not real . . . And then we might finally be able to make some money out of the place. But no one ever listens to me.'

I nodded to Freddie. 'Can I talk to you for a minute?'

'You see!' said Arthur.

She made a shushing gesture, blew him a kiss and then moved a little away so the two of us could talk privately.

'Something bothering you, Ishmael? Love the name . . .'

'It's just that out of everyone here, you seem the least intimidated by this house. You didn't even seem that bothered by the unpleasant atmosphere earlier.'

She smiled. 'I've felt all kinds of things during my explorations into the darker corners of the world. It's usually just your own subconscious responding to cues you haven't realized you noticed, and making you pay attention. Besides, I took precautions before I set out this evening. I am protected by the clear white light.'

'Did you bring enough for all of us?' I said politely.

Freddie laughed. 'It's a spiritual thing. A defence we can all call on in times of trouble.'

'Last chance to come clean,' I said. 'Do you really believe in ghosts?'

'Of course!' said Freddie, genuinely surprised I could still ask such a question. 'You can, and should, argue about exactly what it is people see when they see a ghost, but you can't say that people don't see ghosts, because they do. And always have done. The venerable historian Pliny wrote about a haunted villa in ancient Rome. Encounters with ghosts have been recorded in all countries and cultures. Of course, the nature of the ghost does tend to change, according to the place and the period. They used to be all about revealing hidden crimes or treasures; then they were restless souls, agonizing over unavenged murders or unfinished business. And in Victorian times they were all about making contact with the other side . . .'

'What kind of ghost do you believe in?' I said.

She grinned and elbowed me in the ribs. 'All of them. It saves time.'

'We can start whenever you're ready,' Tom said loudly. 'My cameras are locked in position, and all the microphones are live.'

I nodded my thanks to Freddie and moved over to Tom.

'You're a ghost-hunter,' I said. 'What do you think ghosts are?'

'Could be a stone tape,' he said immediately. 'An emotional event so powerful it imprints itself on its surroundings, producing a recording that can play itself back under the right conditions. Other hauntings could be the result of a timeslip, a window through which we can observe the past. And sometimes ghosts are just an hallucination. Put someone under enough emotional pressure and distress, and they'll see anything. In my opinion, any of these scenarios are easier to believe than that the dead come back from the grave just to wander around putting the wind up people.'

'At last,' I said, 'someone sensible I can talk to.'

'Ghosts are just a natural phenomenon we don't understand yet,' said Tom. 'They'll probably turn out to be something along the lines of electromagnetic energy, like ball lightning.'

'Ah,' I said. 'And you were doing so well . . .'

'I think I'd feel a lot easier if I could believe in such

straightforward theories,' Freddie said loudly. 'But given all the varieties of weird stuff I've encountered in my time, I need magic to make sense of them.'

'You'd be better off putting your faith in science!' said Tom.

'Magic is just science seen from the other direction,' said Freddie.

Tom looked at her. 'That makes no sense at all.'

'I like it,' said Arthur.

'You would,' said Tom.

Penny looked steadily at Freddie. 'If you ever did meet an actual ghost, what would you do?'

'Talk to it, of course!' said Freddie. 'Ask it questions.'

'What kind of questions?' I said.

She laughed, a little self-consciously. 'Oh, the usual ones, I suppose. What comes next? What's waiting for us? I used to be so sure I knew all the answers, going to church with the family every Sunday . . . But as I grew older, and saw more of the world, and followed my instincts into some pretty strange places, the more I learned, the less sure I became. About anything. It would be good to be able to go straight to the horse's mouth and get some clear answers.'

'But could you trust them?' I said. 'If ghosts are just people – well, people lie all the time.'

'What reasons could the dead have to lie to the living?' said Freddie.

'That's one of the first things I'd want to find out,' I said.

There was a pause, as everyone thought about that.

'I think I'd know the truth when I heard it,' Freddie said finally.

'Aren't ghosts at least proof of life after death?' said Penny.

'Only if they're what they seem to be,' I said.

Penny gave me a hard look. 'For someone who doesn't believe in ghosts, you do seem to have given the matter a lot of thought.'

'Know thy enemy,' I said.

'Before we begin the seance, I have a few things to say,' said Tom.

'Never knew a scientist who didn't,' said Freddie.

Tom cleared his throat meaningfully, and we all dutifully paid attention. Apart from Lynn, who was still lost in her own thoughts.

'If anything should happen during the seance, it will be recorded,' said Tom. 'So stay where the cameras can see you, and speak as clearly as you can, for the mikes. And, please, watch your language. I shall be showing this recording to the scientific community – if we actually produce something worth watching.'

And then he broke off, as something on his screen caught his eye. The feeds from all four cameras were breaking up and being replaced by darkness or static. One just shut down completely, as though the camera was broken.

'This shouldn't be happening,' Tom said tightly. 'Something must be interfering with the signal. Something unusually powerful.'

'Have you tried turning it off and turning it back on again?' I said.

Tom actually growled at me, without taking his eyes off the screen. He put his laptop down and slapped the side of the screen, and when that didn't work, he picked the laptop up with both hands and shook it. All four feeds immediately stabilized. Tom quickly put the laptop down again.

'Are you sure you're not an engineer?' said Freddie. 'That was only just short of "We're going to need a bigger hammer".'

'Oh, shit . . .' said Tom.

'What?' Arthur said quickly. 'What's gone wrong now?'

Tom scowled at the readings scrolling down the side of his screen. 'The room temperature has dropped again. Another four degrees . . . How could we not have noticed that?'

'Because it might not be the room,' I said. 'It might just be the readings. I don't think we can trust anything in this house.'

'There's nothing wrong with my readings!' said Tom. 'It can't be something in the house affecting us, because we're sealed off in here. The door is closed—'

'And the only window is nailed shut,' said Penny.

'What?' said Arthur. 'How do you know that?'

'Because we looked,' Penny said crushingly.

Arthur peered at the window and appeared to be genuinely upset for the first time.

'Why would anyone want to nail up the window? It's not like anyone wants to get in.'

'Maybe to keep something from getting out,' I said.

There was another long pause as everyone considered the implications of that, and decided they really didn't like them.

Freddie rubbed her hands together. 'It does feel colder in here.'

'There is a theory that ghosts soak up energy from their surroundings, to fuel their manifestations,' said Tom.

'Or maybe it's just cold for the time of year!' said Arthur.

I moved in beside Tom. 'Are your motion-trackers picking up anything?'

He checked his readings. 'Nothing moving anywhere else in the house. Why do you ask?'

'I just wondered whether all of this might be a distraction, to keep us from noticing that something more important was happening somewhere else. Can you expand their range at all?'

'I didn't exactly buy them off the shelf,' Tom said reluctantly. 'I had to teach myself how to work them, through trial and error.'

'Hold it; go back,' said Penny. 'Just how reliable is all this scientific equipment of yours?'

'It's the best I could get for the money!' said Tom. 'Specialist ghost-hunting tech doesn't come cheap, you know.'

'Have you ever recorded anything that you could actually show to people?' said Arthur.

Tom kept his gaze fixed on the screen. Possibly because that made it easier for him to lecture us.

'I have had some strange experiences, but never anything I could be sure of. The problem is, the human mind is hard-wired to find patterns in things. That's why people see shapes in clouds or inkblots. But cameras only record what's actually in front of them. If I see something, and then see it on the screen, and then see it again on the recording afterwards, then I can believe in it. And present it as proof to other people.'

'Seeing a recording is believing?' said Penny.

'If you like,' said Tom.

'I think I've been very patient,' Lynn said loudly, 'but it really is time we got this seance under way. All of you want answers, and this is the best way to get them.'

'All right!' said Freddie. 'Let's get this show on the road!'

Arthur glowered about him. 'I am not holding anyone's hand. I do not do the touchy-feely thing with strangers.'

'I'm not a stranger,' said Freddie.

'You're just strange,' said Arthur.

'And you love it,' said Freddie.

Arthur smiled in spite of himself and then looked reluctantly at Lynn. 'If we must, we must . . . All right, then, house-cleanser, how do we get this started? Do you need to summon up an Indian spirit guide?'

Lynn surprised us all with a brief bark of laughter. 'I'm sorry, Arthur, but that is so last century. And anyway, I'm a psychic, not a medium. I don't do trances, and I don't pass on messages from the great beyond. I merely function as a contact point between this world and the next. I'm going to try to reach out to whatever is in the house with us, and ask it to make itself known to us. Come and sit next to me, Arthur. Your family connections will help me make contact.'

Arthur didn't look at all happy about that, but he shrugged quickly and dropped down on the floor beside her. Lynn patted his arm comfortingly, and while she was busy doing that, I sat down on her other side, settling myself firmly into position before she could object. If she was going to do anything, I wanted to be right there watching it happen. Lynn smiled at me coolly.

'Thank you, Ishmael. Your disbelief will help balance me. Just don't be alarmed by anything you see or hear.'

'I'll try not to be,' I said.

Penny sat down next to me, and Freddie started to sit down by Arthur, but Tom got there first, because that way he was in the best position to keep a close watch on his screen. Freddie reluctantly sat down between Tom and Penny, closing the circle. She'd barely settled herself before Tom made a quiet but distinctly upset sound.

'What is it, Tom?' said Lynn, showing great patience under the circumstances.

He shot her an uncomfortable look. 'It just occurred to me that if I ever do present these recordings to my peers, they'll all be able to see me taking part *in a seance*. I'll never live it down.'

'You could always edit yourself out,' I said. 'Pixilate your face or something.'

'No,' he said immediately. 'I couldn't compromise the evidence.'

'No one will laugh at you if you're in a position to provide hard evidence of ghostly phenomena,' said Lynn.

Tom nodded reluctantly.

Once Lynn had assured herself that we were all sitting comfortably, she started speaking quite calmly and casually, with none of her usual practised theatrics – as though she was putting the showbusiness routine to one side, so she could concentrate on what mattered. Her heavy Goth makeup suddenly made her seem that much more solemn and determined.

'Every haunted house is really all about death. Loss and grief, heightened emotions and broken hearts. A need to know what comes after, along with an understandable fear of what the answers might be. Strong emotional states allow the human mind to experience far more than it is normally capable of. We have to open our minds to what this house has to show us. So just sit quietly, breathe steadily and let me do all the heavy lifting.'

We sat very still, our shoulders touching. We weren't holding hands, but we might as well have been. I could feel agitation in Penny's shoulder, and a surprising amount of tension in Lynn's. There was a definite feeling of connection between everyone in the circle.

'I don't read minds,' said Lynn. 'I read places. I place myself in tune with my surroundings, through practised mental disciplines, so I can see what lies beneath the surface of the world. I am going to try to persuade whatever is here to talk to us, but if it can't or won't, or if it proves hostile, I will perform a cleansing. Either by opening a door, so the inhabiting presence can move on, or by compelling it to leave, with an exorcism. Not through commands and abuse, as in the Roman ritual, but by dispersing any dark emotions through positive reinforcement.'

'How can anyone who looks like such a Goth sound so much like a hippy?' said Arthur.

'Practice,' said Lynn. 'Don't worry, Arthur. Once the presence is gone, this house will be just a house again.'

'I should be able to help you with that,' said Freddie.

'Hush, Freddie, please,' said Lynn, not even looking at her. This was Lynn's moment, and she had no intention of sharing the spotlight with anyone. 'I can't allow anything that might interfere with my concentration.'

'I'm here if you need me,' said Freddie, entirely unmoved. 'Don't be afraid to ask for backup if you need it.'

'Have you had much success, Lynn, in cleansing haunted houses?' said Penny.

'I prefer to call them spiritually troubled locations,' said Lynn. 'The other term carries too much emotional baggage.'

'Oh, hell,' said Arthur. 'Political correctness in a haunted house. Where will it end?'

'I have enjoyed a number of successes,' said Lynn. 'Many of which I have discussed with the local media, who have always been very supportive.'

'Only because you always provide the editors with suitably sexy photos and a good sound bite,' said Arthur. 'And yet somehow you're always very evasive in your interviews, when it comes to providing actual names and places.'

'The privacy of the people involved has to come first,' said Lynn. 'They've been through enough, without being persecuted by an overbearing media.'

'Even when I was able to track people down,' said Arthur, refusing to be stopped or sidetracked, 'I couldn't find anyone prepared to go on the record and confirm you actually did anything to help them.'

Lynn looked at him directly for the first time. 'Why are you so fascinated by my career, Arthur?'

'I became interested after I discovered you only gave my paper stories as long as the editor agreed to use the promotional information you provided,' said Arthur. 'You were just using the *Herald* for free advertising.'

'People need to know how to find me,' Lynn said calmly. 'And, Arthur, people often don't like to talk about their encounters with the hidden world. They just want to move on and forget the bad things ever happened. Particularly when they're being ambushed by an unsympathetic journalist with an agenda.'

'What qualifications do you have, to do what you do?' Arthur shot back.

'I do my best to help, when no one else can,' said Lynn. 'What else is there?'

I shared a glance with Penny. Lynn might be a confidence trickster, only in it for the money, or she could be well-meaning but deluded. Either way, I wasn't sure what she hoped to achieve with a seance.

Arthur glowered at Lynn, and she stared calmly back at him, refusing to be browbeaten.

'I don't believe in ghosts or haunted houses, or anything spiritual,' Arthur said flatly.

'That's all right,' said Lynn. 'They believe in you.'

'And I don't believe there's anything supernatural inhabiting this house!' Arthur said forcefully. 'The weird stories didn't start appearing until long after my ancestors had left the country and weren't around to defend themselves. It was all just malicious gossip, which Malcolm Welles may or may not have deserved. The legend about this house only started because people like ghost stories!'

'But no one has ever claimed to have seen a ghost here,' I said. 'And the locals don't seem at all fond of the stories. They sound traumatized, just from having to live so close to Harrow House.'

'And what about all the things we've experienced since we entered this house?' said Tom.

'Nothing but mass hysteria,' said Arthur.

'I think you need more than six people to qualify as a mass,' Tom said mildly.

'He's got you there, Arthur,' said Freddie.

He sniffed loudly. Freddie reached across to pat his arm

comfortingly, but he wouldn't look at her. Freddie shrugged and turned away to address the circle.

'Before we begin the seance, I think we should all tell a ghost story! It'll help put us in the proper frame of mind. And I don't mean stories you've heard; I mean your own personal experiences with ghosts.'

'How can you be sure we've all had one?' I said.

'Because everyone has,' said Freddie. 'Lynn, I know you're eager to get the seance started – so am I – but I really think we need to do this first.'

Lynn sighed quietly. 'Very well, if you think it will help.'

'Who wants to go first?' said Freddie.

Surprisingly, Tom leaned forward. 'I can tell you about something that happened to me, a few years ago. I woke up in the early hours of the morning. I was lying alone in bed, but I wasn't the only one there. An invisible figure was leaning over me, holding me down. I couldn't see it, but I could feel its weight. Feel its hands on my arms, holding me in place. Feel the individual fingers, as they dug into my flesh.

'But I wasn't scared; I was furious. I fought the invisible presence, throwing all my weight against it, determined to break free. After a few moments I was able to throw it off and sit bolt upright. The sense of an invisible presence was gone, just like that. And I thought, *I know what that was! That was sleep paralysis!*'

He smiled triumphantly around the circle. 'I'd read an article on the subject, not long before. While we're sleeping, a part of our brain paralyses us, so we won't physically act out what we do in dreams. But sometimes we wake up too quickly, and the paralysis lingers on for a moment. And in that half-awake state, our brain manufactures an explanation; like an invisible presence, holding us down.

'But if I hadn't read that particular article, I might be telling you a very different story.'

He smiled around the circle as we all applauded politely. It had been a pretty good effort.

'My account is rather different,' said Freddie. 'I'd been called in to investigate a problem with a small shop, in an old country town. The owner had reported strange happenings that he was beginning to find disturbing. The shop itself turned out to be very old, with parts of it dating all the way back to the thirteenth century, and the interior was fairly basic – stone walls, a ground floor for the shop, and a second floor that the owner used as a stock room. He told me that sometimes, when he was in the place on his own, he would hear footsteps moving about upstairs. But when he went up to check, there was never anyone there. He didn't want to believe in ghosts, but what other explanation could there be?

'I asked the owner to leave me alone in the shop, and he did. I walked back and forth, getting a feel for the place, and sure enough, I heard footsteps on the floor above. Someone walking about very quietly, as though they didn't want to be noticed. But it didn't take me long to work out what was going on. The shop consisted of a wooden floor, connected by a set of wooden stairs to a second wooden floor. I was hearing my own footsteps, which had travelled up the stairs and reverberated in the upper floor! It was nothing but a delayed echo. Not a ghost at all.'

She smiled as we applauded, and looked to me to continue, but I shook my head steadily.

'Two stories, and no real ghost? I think you're undermining your own case.'

'Then tell us your story,' said Freddie.

'I don't have one,' I said. 'I have never seen anything to make me believe in ghosts. And I've been around.'

'Oh, he has,' said Penny. 'Really. You have no idea.'

'Do you have a story?' said Tom.

'No,' said Penny. 'I was kind of hoping that tonight would turn out to be my ghost story.'

'How about you, Arthur?' said Freddie. 'Our confirmed sceptic . . . Do you have anything to contribute?'

'Yes,' said Arthur, just a bit unexpectedly. 'I have a story. It doesn't have an ending, or an explanation; it's just something that happened to me when I was six years old.

'Like Tom, I woke up in the early hours of the morning. It was summer, and the room was full of light. I was just lying there, waiting to go back to sleep, when a dark human shape walked out of the wall to my left, crossed in front of my bed and then disappeared through the right-hand wall.

'Now, when you're that age, you tend to just accept things. So I waited for a while, to see if the figure would show up again, and when it didn't, I went back to sleep. In the morning, I told my mother what I'd seen. She said it must have been my father, looking in to check I was all right. But I said no. Then it must have been a dream, she said. She was starting to sound a bit impatient, so I just nodded and got on with my cornflakes. But I knew it wasn't a dream.

'What was it, really? I don't know. I don't have any answer for you. But that's my story.'

'But . . . after an experience like that, how can you say you don't believe in ghosts?' said Penny.

'Because I don't know what I saw,' said Arthur. 'I never saw anything like it again. And after all these years, how can I even be sure that I'm remembering it correctly?'

'Denial isn't just a river in Egypt,' said Tom.

'I'm a journalist,' Arthur said coldly. 'I won't accept any story that isn't based on provable facts.'

I looked at Lynn. 'I suppose you have a story.'

'Of course,' said Lynn. 'I was once called upon to cleanse an old Norman church in Wiltshire—'

'Oh, not that one!' said Arthur. 'You've told that story half a dozen times in interviews, but I haven't been able to find a church anywhere in the whole of the West Country that fits the details you gave. Like a lot of your stories, it doesn't stand up to close examination.'

'I know you've been looking into my past, Arthur,' said Lynn. 'I have friends, who tell me things. There are always going to be people who are jealous of those with gifts. What you've been hearing are just their attempts to bring me down.'

She didn't sound disturbed or even embarrassed by Arthur's claims. His face flushed angrily.

'I will prove you're a fraud,' he said flatly. 'No matter how long it takes. People talk to me, too.'

'I've had to face this kind of disbelief all through my career,' Lynn said quietly. 'It's often hard for people to accept the kind of things I've experienced. Most prefer to believe in the things that comfort them. But it doesn't matter what convictions you cling to, Arthur; this house will make a believer out of you.'

He subsided, reluctantly. Lynn looked steadily round the circle.

'If everybody is quite ready . . . then I'll begin.'

She delved into her wicker bag and brought out several paper sachets. She tore them open one at a time, and sprinkled coloured powders over our heads, with what might or might not have been mystical gestures. We all just sat there politely and let her get on with it. I wondered if we were all going to end up with multi-coloured dandruff, and suppressed an urge to shake my head vigorously. I smiled politely at Lynn.

'I knew aromatherapy would turn up at some point.'

'I have a degree in organic chemistry,' she said calmly. 'I understand these things. It's all about establishing the right atmosphere. Speaking of which . . .' She reached into her wicker bag again and brought out a thermos and a stack of paper cups. She opened the thermos and poured hot steaming liquid into one cup after another.

'Just a little herbal tea,' she said. 'To help settle everyone's nerves.'

The room was cold enough to make a hot drink seem very appealing. Lynn passed a hand over each cup in a blessing, before passing it on.

'May God bless all here and look kindly on our undertaking in this matter.'

It wasn't much of a blessing, and I particularly didn't like the use of the word *undertaking*. Not that I'm superstitious; just sensibly cautious. Which is why I waited for the others to try the tea before I did. It was pleasant enough.

Arthur looked around the room, frowning. 'Is it just me or does it feel even colder in here?'

'Probably just the tea,' said Freddie, sipping hers loudly.

Tom glanced over at his monitor screen and sat up straight. 'The temperature has dropped again! I don't believe it!'

He started to get to his feet, only to sit quickly back down again when Lynn glared at him.

'You stay right where you are, Tom! The circle must not be broken. Not after all the trouble I've gone to, establishing a proper communion between us. Now – if everyone could please finish their tea and pass me back the cups – it's time we got started.'

We all finished our tea, made appropriately grateful noises and handed the cups back to Lynn. She tucked them away in her wicker bag, along with the thermos, and smiled quickly round the circle.

'First rule of haunted houses: don't litter.'

'First rule?' I said.

'Well, it might not be the first,' said Lynn. 'But it's definitely up there in the top ten. Now, everyone, please hold hands.'

'I knew that was coming,' Arthur growled.

'Just pretend it's me,' said Freddie.

Arthur smiled and then pretended he hadn't.

We all took hold of each other's hands. Everyone looked a bit uncomfortable, but no one said anything. Lynn raised her head and addressed the room in a friendly, confident tone.

'I am speaking to any entity present . . . Please make yourself known to this circle and explain to us why you are feeling so troubled. We can help you. You only have to tell us what's wrong.'

I was expecting more, but she just stopped talking and sat there. Waiting. We all sat very still, gripping each other's hands tightly. As much for mutual support as anything. Everyone was breathing a little faster than usual. We were all sitting so close I could hear everyone's heartbeats, like so many muffled drums, and even the harsh rustling of their clothes. But I couldn't hear anything else.

Suddenly, the overbearing feeling of dread and horror was back, even stronger than before. Like a terrible weight pressing down on my mind. I looked round the circle and saw the same sense of shock in everyone's face.

'I told you,' said Lynn. Her voice was steady and entirely unmoved. 'We're not alone here. Hello? Who's there? What is it you need, and how can we help? Please, talk to us.'

The door opened on its own. I was sure it had been properly closed, but now the door was swinging slowly out into the room, revealing nothing beyond it but an impenetrable darkness. The hallway should have been visible, but there was only the dark . . . I couldn't see a thing. And I have always been able to see something, even in the darkest and blackest of nights. It felt as if our small room was the only spot of light left in the world, surrounded by an ocean of darkness.

'Nobody move,' Lynn said harshly. 'Don't break the circle! As long as we remain connected, we're protected.'

'But there's nothing out there,' said Tom. 'Nothing at all!'

'We called and we have been answered,' said Lynn. 'Something is here; can't you feel it?'

Penny's hand clamped down on mine. I squeezed it reassuringly. We all sat very still, our eyes fixed on the darkness that filled the doorway. Lynn was right. Something was there, in the dark, watching us. Getting ready to come forward and emerge into the light. And when it did, and we were finally able to see what it was, it was going to be the worst thing in the world. I'd just started to gather my legs under me, so I could get to my feet in a hurry, when Lynn's head came up sharply.

'Did you feel that? There's a presence – here in the room with us!'

'I'm not feeling that!' said Tom. 'Is anyone else feeling that?'

'There's something in the walls,' said Lynn. Her voice had a fey, faraway quality, as though she was dreaming.

'I'm not feeling anything!' said Arthur.

Penny looked at me and shook her head quickly.

Tom craned his neck to make out the readings on his monitor screen. 'There's all kinds of information coming in, but . . . none of it makes any sense! It's like the data is being swamped, by some stronger signal!'

'Don't be afraid!' Freddie said loudly. 'I call on the clear white light, to protect us all!'

'The light can't help you,' said Lynn.

Arthur cried out. He jerked both his hands free in a sudden spasm and then fell backwards until his head hit the floor with a dull thud. He didn't move, staring up at the ceiling with wide fixed eyes. Lynn screamed and scrabbled backwards across the floor. Her feet kicked against Arthur's arm, but he didn't react. I hurried over to kneel at Arthur's side, but I couldn't find any trace of a pulse, and he wasn't breathing. Penny moved in beside me, and I shook my head.

'Arthur?' said Freddie, her voice thick with horror and loss. 'Arthur!'

'I'm sorry,' I said. 'He's dead.'

'How can he be dead?' said Tom.

'I can't find any obvious cause,' I said.

'Look at his face!' said Lynn. 'Isn't it obvious? He died of fright!'

I looked back at the door. It was very firmly shut. As though it had never been open.

FOUR
Unexpected Voices

Lynn started to reach out a hand to Arthur, then she snatched it back and got slowly to her feet. She was shaking, and her eyes were wide and confused. Freddie was already standing up. She wasn't shaking, and her mouth was firm, but she never took her eyes off Arthur. Tom was also up, shaking his head over and over, as though he could deny what was happening. Penny and I got to our feet, but before either of us could say anything, Lynn raised her voice.

'We have to get out of here!'

She started towards the closed door, but Freddie moved quickly to stop her, one hand clamping down hard on her arm. Lynn tried to pull away, but couldn't. She whirled on Freddie.

'Let go of me! What's wrong with you?'

'You are not opening that door,' Freddie said sharply. 'The darkness could still be there, or whatever's in it that killed Arthur.'

Lynn looked at the closed door and swallowed hard. Freddie let go of Lynn, but she didn't move.

'There's nothing on the other side of that door,' I said.

Everyone turned to look at me.

'How can you be so sure, Ishmael?' said Penny.

'Because if there was anything outside, I'd hear it,' I said. 'And I'm not hearing anything.'

'All right, then,' said Tom. 'If you're so sure, you open the door.'

I started forward, and they all fell back to give me plenty of room. Penny wanted to go with me, but I shook my head quickly. Because I have been known to be wrong, on occasion. I stopped before the closed door and listened so hard I could have heard the dust falling, but there was nothing. I took a firm hold on the handle and pulled the door open. The hallway was full of bright electric light, just as it should be – still and quiet and completely empty, all the way to the front door. There was no trace of the darkness we'd seen before, and now that the mood had been broken, I was starting to wonder if it had ever really been there.

I stepped back and indicated the normality of the hall with a wave of my hand. Lynn bolted past me and went running down the hall, heading for the front door. Freddie and Tom hurried after her, not even glancing at me. They'd had enough of the mysteries of Harrow House. They just wanted out. I looked at Penny.

'Did you see what was in the dark that killed Arthur?' she said, her voice entirely steady. 'With those incredible eyes of yours?'

'I didn't see anything,' I said.

'What are we going to do?' said Penny.

'Well, first, we go after the others,' I said. 'Because they might need protecting, and because if Arthur was murdered, they're our best suspects.'

'You think he was murdered?' said Penny.

'Don't you?' I said.

Penny looked at Arthur's body, still lying where it had fallen, and nodded slowly.

'Poor man. No one ever seems to die of natural causes on one of our cases.'

'I know,' I said. 'I'm starting to feel like a jinx.'

She managed a small smile for me. 'We'd better get a move on, or we'll end up chasing the others through the gardens.'

'They're not going anywhere,' I said. 'I had Arthur lock the front door, remember?'

She looked at me admiringly. 'You really do think ahead, don't you?'

'Someone has to.'

We set off down the hall. I kept a watchful eye on the side doors, but neither of them showed any signs of opening. We soon caught up with the others, crowded together before the front door. Lynn had both hands on the handle and was struggling with it for all she was worth, but the door wouldn't budge. Tom pushed her out of the way without even bothering to be polite about it, but he didn't fare any better with the handle. He swore loudly and pounded on the door with his fist. Freddie looked as if she was thinking of trying a punch or two herself. All three of them were so intent on the door that they didn't even notice Penny and I had arrived.

'We're going to need a really good reason to keep them here, Ishmael,' Penny said quietly.

'We have no idea how Arthur died, or why,' I said. 'It could be down to the house, but it's far more likely that one of these people is responsible. So no one is going anywhere, until I understand exactly what happened.'

Penny looked at me. 'It could be dangerous to remain here, Ishmael.'

I shook my head firmly. 'I haven't seen anything to convince me that there's anything threatening about this house.'

'What about the darkness in the doorway?'

'Darkness doesn't kill people.'

Penny nodded reluctantly. 'And healthy young men don't just drop dead for no reason.'

'Not even in supposedly haunted houses,' I said. 'Which is why that door is staying locked.

'How could the hall be so dark,' said Penny, 'when the lights were on the whole time?'

'I'm still working on that,' I said. 'But the darkness did make for one hell of a distraction. I have to wonder what it kept us from noticing, that someone else didn't want us to see.'

Penny smiled suddenly. 'I do love the way your mind works.'

'Years of experience,' I said. 'I've learned the hard way not to trust anything or anybody. Apart from you, of course.'

'Nice save, sweetie,' said Penny.

I cleared my voice loudly, and the three people struggling with the front door jumped as though they'd been stabbed. They spun round to face Penny and me.

'You're not going to force open a door that heavy,' I said. 'They knew how to build things in Victorian times.'

'There must be a back door somewhere,' said Tom, his voice rising in a way that promised something very like hysteria in the near future.

'You would expect that to be the case, wouldn't you?' I said. 'But think about it. The ground floor is made up of just the three rooms, and not one of them possesses another exit. I don't see where else we could look for a back door. There's no kitchen, no storage area and no servants' quarters.'

'Maybe they're all upstairs,' said Penny.

'Even if they are, I doubt we'll find a back door up there,' I said. 'I think Malcolm Welles designed this house to have just the one way in or out.'

'Why would he do that?' said Penny.

'To control the only way people could enter or leave,' I said. 'This was never intended to be just a family home.'

'What else could it be?' said Freddie.

Her voice was steady enough, but her face was grim, all her bonhomie gone with Arthur's death.

'A prison,' Lynn said suddenly. 'To keep whatever is still here from getting out.'

We all thought about that for a moment.

'What about Malcolm's family?' said Penny.

'He doesn't strike me as the kind of man who gave a damn about anything but his own interests,' I said. 'It's always possible the family were never allowed to know what they were sharing their house with.'

'I told you there was something here,' said Lynn. 'Are you ready to admit this house is haunted, after all?'

'Not by ghosts,' I said. 'By something from the past . . . perhaps.'

'Like what?' said Freddie. Her shock was giving way to anger as the frustration of the situation took hold.

'Good question,' I said.

Lynn kicked at the closed front door. 'We're trapped in here! Trapped, with whatever killed Arthur! The house doesn't want us to leave!'

'It's not the house,' I said. 'I had Arthur lock the door, right after we arrived.'

The three of them looked at me as though I was insane.

'Why the hell would you do something so stupid?' said Tom, his voice rising dangerously.

'So we wouldn't be interrupted in our investigation,' I said calmly. 'The keys to the house should still be in Arthur's pockets. I would have told you that if you hadn't just bolted out of the room.'

'Yes . . .' said Freddie. 'You told me the door was locked, earlier on . . .'

Lynn looked at her incredulously. 'Then why didn't you say something?'

'Because I'd forgotten!' said Freddie. And then she stopped herself and frowned. 'How could I forget something like that?'

'Because you're upset, about Arthur,' said Penny.

'Of course I'm upset! But I haven't lost my mind . . . I think this house is messing with our heads.'

Tom fixed me with a cold stare. 'Did you bring the keys with you?'

'No,' I said.

'Why not?' said Lynn.

'Because I thought it was more important to come after you and make sure all of you were OK,' I said. 'But all we have to do is get the keys from Arthur's pocket and unlock the front door, and then we can be on our way. If you're sure that's what you want.'

Freddie looked at me suspiciously. 'Why wouldn't we want to leave? Arthur just died, right in front of us!'

'Yes,' I said. 'He did. Don't you want to know why?'

'Yes,' said Freddie. 'I do.' Her voice was suddenly very cold.

'I just want to get out of here,' said Lynn. 'Before something else happens.'

'Then let's go and get the keys,' I said.

Lynn, Freddie and Tom looked back down the long empty hall, to where the door to the far room was still standing open. None of them looked at all happy about going back to a room with a dead body in it. I gave them some time to make up their minds, but none of them moved.

'I didn't see anything actually dangerous in that room,' I said finally. 'Did any of you?'

There was a slow shaking of heads.

'We all panicked,' I said kindly. 'Which is completely understandable, given the circumstances. But the more I think about

it, the less convinced I am that Arthur's death had anything
to do with this house.'

'He died after the door opened on its own,' said Freddie.
The anger was gone from her voice, replaced by a cold resolve
as she concentrated on the situation. 'He looked at the dark
in the door, and he died.'

'We all looked into the dark,' I said. 'And we're still here
. . . And besides, how could darkness kill anybody?'

'He died of fright!' said Lynn.

'It wasn't that scary,' I said flatly. 'And Arthur was a reporter.
He didn't strike me as someone who scared easily. There could
be all manner of reasons for what happened to him. We don't
know anything about his medical history.'

'You're right,' said Tom. 'Occam's razor: always go for the
simple answer.' He took a deep breath and made a visible
effort to steady himself. 'We've been letting this house get to
us. We need to find those keys.'

'And then get the hell out of here,' said Lynn.

Freddie looked down the hall to the far room. 'I don't like
the idea of leaving Arthur here on his own.'

'He's dead!' said Lynn. 'We can't help him. We have to
help ourselves.'

Freddie glared at her. 'What is wrong with you? Anyone
would think this was your first haunted house.'

Lynn glared right back at her. 'I never saw anyone die right
in front of me before! And I don't want to watch it happen
again.'

Tom looked at her sharply. 'You think that's a possibility?'

'Don't you?' said Lynn.

'Let's get the keys,' I said.

They all nodded, but still none of them moved. In the end,
Penny and I had to lead the way back down the hall, with the
others following on behind. Penny leaned in close, so
she could murmur to me.

'What happens once we've got the keys? If they really are
murder suspects, how do we stop them from leaving?'

'I have something in mind,' I said.

I entered the far room with Penny right beside me, but the
others only got as far as the doorway, then stopped. They stood

bunched together, looking anxiously at Arthur's body to make sure it was still where it had been. And perhaps to reassure themselves that it wasn't about to sit up and call them names for rushing off and leaving him. I knelt down beside Arthur and searched quickly through his jeans pockets. There was no trace of the keys anywhere.

'What's the matter?' Tom said finally, taking a single cautious step into the room.

'He doesn't have the house keys on him,' I said, standing up.

'But . . . we only left him alone for a few moments!' said Freddie.

'He must have them somewhere!' said Lynn.

'That's what I thought,' I said. 'But he doesn't.'

'What could have happened to them?' said Penny.

'Someone must have taken them,' I said.

'Or something got to him,' said Lynn.

We all turned to look at her. Freddie had joined Tom inside the room, but Lynn was still standing in the doorway, staring unblinkingly at Arthur's body. Her heavily made-up face looked more like a mask than usual.

'What do you mean – some*thing*?' said Tom.

'Whatever it is, it doesn't want us to leave this house,' said Lynn.

'Ghosts aren't renowned for picking people's pockets,' Freddie said acidly. 'If whatever's here wanted to stop us leaving, I think it would have done something more . . . dramatic.'

'Taking Arthur's keys feels a lot more like human intervention to me,' I said.

'But there's no one else in the house who could have taken the keys,' said Freddie, frowning.

'The house took them!' Lynn said loudly.

'Oh, do shut up,' said Freddie. She didn't even glance at Lynn, her gaze fixed on Arthur's unmoving form.

'It could be treasure-seekers,' said Penny. 'Someone who got into the house before us, and has been messing with our heads ever since, so we'll leave and they can get on with their search.'

'Someone murdered my Arthur?' said Freddie, her voice suddenly quieter and more dangerous.

Tom was already shaking his head. 'There can't be anyone else here. My motion-trackers would have picked them up.'

'Oh, of course,' said Freddie. 'Because your bits and pieces have proved so reliable this far.'

'What about the undisturbed dust on the floor?' I said to Penny.

'That's so obvious it must be misleading!'

I smiled at her. 'I love the way your mind works.'

'We have to get out of here!' Lynn said loudly. 'This investigation is over, cancelled on account of sudden death. It wasn't any treasure-seeker who killed Arthur. There was no one else in the room but us, and we were all holding each other's hands. The presence I felt killed Arthur, by frightening him to death. And it will kill all of us if we don't get out of here!'

'The front door is locked!' said Freddie.

'Then we need to call for help,' said Lynn.

She got out her phone. Tom and Freddie did, too. They all seemed relieved at having something practical to do. Penny started to reach for her phone, but I caught her eye and shook my head.

'Allow me to remind you all,' I said patiently, 'that Arthur told us earlier it was almost impossible to get a signal up here.'

'But we're in a major city!' said Tom, shaking his phone vigorously. 'We can't be that far from a tower!'

The three of them strode around the room, holding their phones up high and even pressing them against the walls and the nailed-shut window, but they couldn't manage a single bar between them. Penny gave me a hard look.

'This is really not a good time to be looking smug about us being cut off from the rest of the world.'

'I'm just rattling their cages a little,' I said.

'Why would you want to do that?'

'To see what happens.'

'I think I'll stand well back,' said Penny.

One by one the others gave up on their phones. Tom seemed particularly annoyed that his precious technology had failed him again. Freddie looked as if she was just one misjudged comment away from taking out her frustrations on whomever was closest. Lynn looked seriously upset as she put her phone away.

'We're on our own,' she said. 'Trapped in this awful place, with no way out.'

She sounded more than ever like a small child lost in a dark forest. This evening hadn't worked out the way she thought it would. What should have been another triumph had turned on her viciously. Freddie's hands had closed into fists, but every time she glanced at Arthur's body the anger would leave her eyes, replaced by a gleam of unshed tears.

Tom was the last to give up on his phone. He kept trying different things, as though hoping for some last-minute miracle, and then he suddenly stopped and pressed his phone hard against his ear. He stuck a hand in the air, to get our attention.

'What is it?' said Penny. 'Have you got through to someone?'

'I can hear a voice,' he said. And from the way he said it, we could all tell this wasn't a good thing. We all crowded in around Tom as he stood there, listening and frowning.

'Is it . . . Arthur?' said Lynn.

We all looked at her and then turned back to Tom, but he was already shaking his head.

'It's a voice . . . but it doesn't sound right,' he said slowly. 'Like the kind of language you hear in dreams. Words you can't understand, trying desperately to tell us something important . . .' He shuddered suddenly. 'Just the sound of it makes my skin crawl.'

Freddie snatched the phone away from him and pressed it against her own ear. She listened intently and then scowled.

'I can't hear anything.'

She thrust the phone back into Tom's hand, and he listened again.

'It's gone,' he said. He looked at his phone. 'No signal.'

'Maybe there never was,' said Freddie. 'Maybe . . . the house really is trying to talk to us.'

Tom turned off his phone and put it away. Everyone looked at everyone else.

'How could a voice get through, when none of us could get a signal?' said Lynn.

'You're supposed to be the expert when it comes to unexpected voices,' said Freddie.

Lynn looked at her coldly. 'Phones are science. I don't do science.'

Tom went over to his monitor screen.

'All the readings are in the normal range,' he said slowly. 'Nothing to suggest anything out of the ordinary.' He looked back at us. 'Lynn is right. We can't stay here. Whatever's in this house almost certainly killed Arthur, and it might kill again . . . Maybe we could smash the window, get out that way.'

'I already checked it,' said Freddie. 'Dozens of nails, a heavy wooden frame and really thick glass. You'd need a battering ram just to make a dent in it. And I'd be willing to bet the upstairs windows have been treated just the same. Malcolm Welles wasn't taking any chances.'

'Staying here isn't that bad an option,' I said. 'All we have to do is get through the night and wait for the people coming to pick us up in the morning. They can smash in the front door and let us out.'

Everyone thought about that.

'We should be safe enough here, as long as we stick together,' said Tom.

'Safe?' said Freddie. 'Arthur died in this room!'

'We can always barricade the door,' said Tom.

'You think that will keep the dark out?' said Freddie.

'I won't stay in the same room as a dead body!' said Lynn, her voice rising dangerously.

We all looked at Arthur, still lying on his back where he'd fallen. We hadn't even got around to arranging him decorously or closing his eyes. Lynn only looked at him for a moment, before turning her face away.

'Why are you so bothered by a dead man?' Freddie said bluntly. 'You talk to the dead all the time, don't you?'

'That's different,' said Lynn. 'I deal in spirits, not . . . remains.'

'We're safer in here than anywhere else,' said Tom. 'We have the cameras to watch over us, and motion-trackers to warn of anyone approaching.'

'None of that helped Arthur,' said Freddie.

'My instruments can also provide a complete record of everything that happens here!' said Tom.

'You mean in case none of us survives to tell the story?' said Lynn.

'You had to go there, didn't you?' said Freddie.

'This room could be the only really safe location in Harrow House,' said Penny.

Freddie looked at her sharply. 'What makes you think that?'

'The darkness was able to fill that doorway,' said Penny. 'But it couldn't enter the room.'

'I felt something in here with us!' said Lynn.

'You're the only one who did,' said Freddie. 'And you weren't in the calmest frame of mind.'

'The darkness didn't move one inch beyond the doorway,' said Penny.

'Perhaps just the presence of my instruments was enough to keep it out,' said Tom.

'Or my protections,' said Freddie.

'We can't be sure the dark had anything to do with Arthur's death,' I said.

'We can't be sure it didn't,' said Tom.

'I am not staying in here with a dead body!' Lynn said loudly. 'Couldn't you at least move it to another room?'

'I don't think he's going to get up and bother anyone,' I said.

'Are you sure about that?' said Lynn.

We all looked at the body. It didn't move.

'If Arthur could get up, he'd have done it by now,' said Freddie. 'He would have thought it was funny.'

'He smells bad!' said Lynn.

'I'm afraid that's what happens when people die,' I said. 'Everything just lets go . . .'

Tom looked at me sharply 'How do you know so much about dead bodies?'

'Penny and I have had some experience in that area,' I said.

'I always knew there was something peculiar about you two,' said Tom. 'What are you, really?'

'We're security,' I said.

And they all just nodded and accepted that. *Security* is one
of those magic words that people tend not to challenge, if only
because they just know they won't like the answers.

'I suppose we could put the body in another room,'
said Tom.

'I think the police would want everything left just the way
it is,' I said. 'So as not to disturb the crime scene.'

'What crime?' said Lynn. 'You think they're going to arrest
the house?'

'But if it wasn't the house,' said Penny, 'someone here must
have killed Arthur.'

They all looked at her and then at each other. I could see
the new idea taking hold in their minds.

'No one here had any reason to kill Arthur,' said Tom. 'And
anyway, none of us even touched him. He just collapsed
and died.'

'For no reason,' Freddie said slowly.

'Either someone moves him or I'll go to another room
and stay there on my own,' Lynn said stubbornly.

'That might not be safe,' I said.

'I don't care!'

I looked at Tom, and he shrugged.

'My cameras recorded the moment of Arthur's death.
That should be enough for the police. We can shift him,
between us.'

'No,' Freddie said immediately. 'You stay where you are,
Tom, and watch your screen. I'll help carry him. So I can
be sure he gets treated with some dignity.'

Tom shrugged. I took Arthur by the shoulders, and Freddie
took his legs, and between us we got him off the floor easily
enough. He was heavy; the dead always are. But the living
always have their way. Freddie and I carried Arthur out of
the room, down the hall and into the left-hand room. We then
settled him in a chair, arranging him so that he seemed to be
just sitting comfortably. Freddie closed Arthur's eyes, with a
gentle touch.

'So he won't know he's in the dark, when we close the
door,' she said.

She caressed his cheek once and then strode out of the room

without looking back. I followed her out and closed the door carefully. Not because I thought Arthur was likely to get up and go wandering around, but so I'd be sure to hear if anyone tried to get to the body and destroy any evidence that might be on it.

Freddie and I walked back to the far room. Lynn and Tom didn't ask any questions. I looked at Penny to see if anything interesting had happened while I was gone, but she just shook her head. Lynn was curled up in her big chair again, her arms wrapped tightly about her as she stared at nothing. Tom was staring at his screen, as though hoping it might yet provide some answers. Freddie chose a chair as far away from Lynn as she could get, and dropped heavily into it. She looked at the spot where Arthur's body had been, but still didn't shed a tear. I closed the door, picked up the heaviest chair I could find and jammed it against the door. Tom looked round from his screen.

'Expecting company?'

'Just being careful,' I said.

'You really think a chair will be enough to keep out whatever's in this house?' said Tom.

'Better than nothing,' I said. I went over to join him. 'Call up the recording of Arthur's death. I want to see exactly what happened.'

'You were right there with us,' said Tom.

'But like the rest of you, I was distracted by the darkness in the doorway,' I said. 'Show me.'

'It was bad enough watching him die the first time,' said Lynn from the depths of her chair. 'I don't want to see it again.'

'Then look away,' I said.

Freddie turned around in her chair, studying me rather than the screen.

'How do you think Arthur died, security man?'

'I don't know yet,' I said. 'But it is possible we might have missed something the first time round. Something important.'

Tom shrugged, found the right moment and set the recording in motion. We all watched the seance and the events leading up to the door full of dark. It was oddly affecting to see Arthur being so animated, with no sense of what was about to happen.

I watched the others watch him. Lynn was leaning forward in her chair, fascinated in spite of herself. Tom seemed more interested in the readings on his screen. Freddie never once took her eyes off Arthur. Penny watched me, to see if I would spot something that everyone else missed.

But I didn't.

Once it was over, and Arthur had died again, I told Tom to run the recording a second time, but it didn't help. I even had Tom zoom in for a close up on Arthur's face, so I could study him carefully as he died. I watched his jaw drop and his eyes widen, and then he just fell backwards. There wasn't enough time for him to feel shock or pain or horror. I was pretty sure he was dead before he hit the floor. Freddie turned her face away, and I nodded for Tom to shut down the recording. The camera feeds filled the screen again, showing us staring at each other from four different angles.

'I told you,' Lynn said dully. 'Arthur was killed by the dark. He saw something in it that we didn't, and the sheer horror of it stopped his heart.'

'He didn't look scared to me,' said Penny.

'It could have been just a normal heart attack, I suppose,' said Tom.

'Of course it wasn't a heart attack!' said Freddie. 'Not at his age!'

'It must have been something like that!' said Tom. 'What else could it have been?'

'It was the house,' said Lynn.

'Hold it!' said Tom.

All four camera feeds had cut out simultaneously, leaving nothing but a screen full of buzzing static. And then something started pinging loudly.

'What is that?' said Penny.

'It's the motion-trackers,' said Tom, leaning in close to study the readings still running down the side of his screen. 'But this can't be right . . . The trackers are saying they're picking up movements all over the house! You'd need an invading army to set off this many responses. And . . . wait a minute, wait a minute . . . All the environmental readings are off the scale!'

And then the camera feeds returned, the readings settled down and the motion-trackers shut up.

'What did you do, Tom?' said Penny.

'I didn't do anything,' he said numbly. He looked hurt that his precious instruments had turned on him.

'What was the point of all that?' said Freddie.

'To send us a message?' said Tom.

'Like the voice on the phone,' said Penny.

'I was right,' said Lynn. 'This house is trying to talk to us.'

'Or . . . someone in this house is messing with Tom's equipment, to distract us,' I said. 'To keep us from noticing something else that's going on.'

'Like what?' said Lynn.

'I don't know,' I said reasonably. 'I was distracted.'

'If we can't trust my instruments, then that means we're not protected by them,' said Tom.

Freddie sniffed. 'Like we ever were . . .'

'We should just leave,' Lynn said forcefully. 'Do whatever it takes to get the hell out of Harrow House, while we still can.'

Tom turned away from his screen and fished around in one of his suitcases. He finally produced a really big hammer – the kind you choose when you think a job might start fighting back.

'I am going back down the hall to beat the shit out of the front door's lock or its hinges, until something falls apart,' he announced loudly. 'Anyone who wants to come with me is welcome, as long as they stay out of my way.'

'Sounds like a plan to me,' said Freddie, heaving herself out of her chair with the light of battle in her eyes. 'I have had enough of this house. It killed my Arthur.'

Lynn got to her feet too, and then all three of them looked at Penny and me. I didn't even try to argue with them. They were in no mood to listen, and I couldn't be sure that they were wrong. This was the only place in the house where something bad had happened. Tom gestured at the barricaded door.

'Are you going to move that chair or just stand there and sulk?'

I hauled the chair away, opened the door and stood back.

'Give it your best shot, Tom. Show that front door no mercy.
If it doesn't work out, you can always come back. I'll keep a
light burning.'

Lynn looked at me incredulously. 'You aren't seriously
thinking of staying here? After everything that's happened?'

'*Because* of everything that's happened,' I said. 'I'm not
leaving until I've got some answers.'

'The house hates us and wants us dead,' said Lynn. 'What
more do you need to know?'

'It must be wonderful to be so sure of things,' I said. 'I
haven't been sure about anything that's happened since we
first set foot inside Harrow House.'

'Arthur died,' said Freddie. 'You can be sure of that.'

'And I have no intention of joining him,' said Tom. 'I'll be
back for my stuff in the morning. When it's light.'

He strode out into the hall, hefting his hammer, with Lynn
and Freddie right behind him. Penny and I stood together in
the doorway to watch them go. There was a new confidence
in Tom's stride now that he had something useful to do. Lynn
and Freddie just seemed pleased that someone had made a
decision.

'You'd better go after them,' I said to Penny.

'Why?' said Penny. 'They look as if they know what they're
doing.'

'I don't think Malcolm Welles would have put his trust
in the kind of door that could be defeated by something as
simple as a hammer,' I said. 'So stand back, watch and listen.
Just in case one of them says something interesting when it
all goes wrong.'

'You are so sharp you'll cut yourself one of these days,'
said Penny. 'Or, more probably, someone else. What am I
supposed to be listening for?'

'I think you'll know it when you hear it,' I said. 'While
you're gone, I'll give this room a good going over. A man
died here, and I want to know why.'

'Of course you do,' said Penny. 'You always feel responsible when someone dies on your watch. Even when it's
obviously not your fault.'

She kissed me quickly and set off down the hall.

Left alone in the room, I looked under every chair, checked every piece of furniture, and even took a quick peek behind all the paintings, very definitely including the portrait of Malcolm Welles. Finally, I tested the nailed-shut window with my more-than-human strength. The nails made awful straining sounds in the heavy wooden frame, but they wouldn't budge. I went back to where we'd held the seance, and knelt down next to where Arthur's body had been. There wasn't a single drop of blood on the bare floorboards, but I could still smell his death on the air. And that was when Arthur appeared before me, standing on the spot where he'd died. I stood up quickly and stared at him, and he glared right back at me.

'What the hell just happened?' he said heatedly.

It took me a moment before I could say anything. 'Damned if I know. Arthur . . . is that you?'

'Of course it's me!'

Arthur looked round the room, while I studied him carefully. He looked perfectly normal, completely solid and very real. Except I couldn't hear his heartbeat or his breathing, and his clothes didn't rustle when he moved. And he had no scent. He turned around suddenly and caught me looking at him.

'What is the matter with you?' he said sharply. 'Why are you looking at me like I owe you money?'

'I think it's more a question of what's the matter with you?' I said. 'I hate to be the one to break it to you, Arthur, but you are quite definitely dead. We all saw you die, right where you're standing. Freddie and I had to carry your body to another room, because it was upsetting the others.'

'I died?' said Arthur. He sounded more puzzled than upset. 'I felt this sudden pain in my chest and I couldn't seem to get my breath, and then . . . I died?'

'I'm afraid so,' I said. 'I checked you over very carefully; you had no vital signs at all.'

'Are you telling me I'm a ghost?' said Arthur. 'That I'm the one haunting Harrow House?'

'Looks like it,' I said. 'Loath though I am to admit it. I don't believe in ghosts.'

'Neither do I,' said Arthur. He looked at me closely. 'Are you all right? Only you've gone a bit pale.'

'I think I'm in shock.'

'Well, don't have a heart attack, or there'll be two of us standing here wondering why we're not breathing.'

I prodded him in the chest with a finger and my hand just kept on going, sinking into his chest until it disappeared up to the wrist. Arthur didn't move, staring down at my arm. I couldn't feel anything, so I waved my hand back and forth through his body without meeting any resistance. I pulled my hand out and looked at it.

'Are you quite finished?' Arthur said coldly.

'Yes,' I said.

'Convinced?'

'Yes.'

'Then don't ever do that again.'

'Sorry,' I said.

'So . . . I really am dead.' Arthur shook his head slowly. 'I'm dead, and I'm a ghost. Definitely not what I expected when I allowed myself to be bullied into visiting Harrow House at last. I can't be dead . . . I'm too young to be dead!' He glared at me. 'How did this happen?'

I had to raise an eyebrow at that. 'Don't you know?'

'No! One moment I was sitting there in the circle, trying to work out what's up with the darkness in the doorway, then the lights go out, and the next thing I know I'm standing here looking at you. Wait a minute . . . You just said you moved my body. What was wrong with it?'

'The smell was starting to upset the others,' I said as kindly as I could.

'Typical,' said Arthur. 'Even when I'm dead, I don't get any respect.'

'I can show you where we put you,' I said. 'If you want.'

'No,' Arthur said quickly. 'I don't think I'm ready to see that yet. Was I . . . disfigured?'

'Not in the least,' I said. 'You just collapsed and died. The others think it might have been a heart attack.'

'Are they crazy? I'm young! Young! I go running every weekend!' He stopped suddenly and looked at me narrowly. 'You don't think that it was a heart attack, do you?'

'I think it's far more likely you were murdered,' I said

steadily. 'Though I'm still working on the how, why and who.'

'Maybe that's why I've come back as a ghost,' said Arthur. 'OK, I feel weird, saying that out loud. I really can't get my head around the idea that I'm dead, and I'm still here.'

'I can understand that,' I said. 'I really don't believe in ghosts.'

He glared at me. 'You even try to wave your arm through me again and I will poltergeist your arse through a wall.'

'You can do that?' I said.

'You want to find out the hard way?'

'Not really,' I said. 'All right, you're a ghost. Where do we go from here?'

'Beats the hell out of me,' said Arthur. 'Are you positive I was murdered?'

'I don't have any hard evidence,' I said. 'I suppose it could have been natural causes, or some phenomenon in the house that we don't properly understand yet, or . . .'

'You don't sound very sure of anything!'

'I'm not,' I said. 'I'm having to make major adjustments in my thinking just to talk to you without losing my cool big time. I've seen all kinds of weird stuff before, but . . .'

'What kind of weird stuff?' Arthur said immediately.

'Vampires, werewolves, psychic assassins . . .'

'Seriously?'

'Yes.'

'Damn! The biggest story of my life – and I'm too dead to do anything about it.' Arthur fumed for a moment and then shrugged unhappily. 'You're not the only one who's having problems dealing with this. I have just realized that I can't feel the floor under my feet, and that is seriously weirding me out. I'm dead, and I'm a ghost . . . I suppose I'm going to have to start giving some serious thought to the afterlife now. Heaven and Hell, and all that. I know it's a bit late, but I always thought I'd have more time to make up my mind. I'm only twenty-five! I mean, I was. And now I'll never be twenty-six. All the things I was going to do . . .'

For a moment I thought he might fall apart, and I had no idea what I could say that would help, but somehow he found the strength to carry on. I was impressed. I wasn't sure I could have done the same, in his circumstances. He looked at me thoughtfully.

'Do you have any idea who might have killed me?'

'Almost certainly one of the people sitting in the seance with you,' I said. 'If only because they had the best opportunity. Though we have been arguing about whether there might be other people hiding somewhere else in the house . . .'

Arthur actually brightened up a little. 'The treasure! They could be looking for the hidden treasure!'

'That is traditional in a situation like this,' I said. 'Are you saying there really is treasure?'

Arthur nodded quickly. 'Could be . . . There are all kinds of stories about what happened to Malcolm Welles's fortune. It disappeared the same time he did. Certainly none of it ever ended up with my side of the family. There was a lot of gossip at the time that he'd left something valuable in the house. My ancestors practically tore the place apart looking for it. Treasure-hunting was about the only thing that could make people strong enough to stand being in this house for a while. But no one ever found anything, so eventually they just gave up.

'Professional treasure-hunters took it in turns to break into the house after that, to look for themselves, but they never found anything either. Some of them came stumbling out half mad, and some never came out at all. Word got around, and the criminal types decided there were safer ways to get rich quick. No one's even tried to dig up the grounds for decades. But perhaps there really is a treasure here, after all! Didn't Freddie say something about ghosts coming back to reveal where treasures were hidden, as well as to complain about being murdered?'

'She did,' I said.

'So just by being here I'm covering all the usual bases.' Arthur stopped and met my gaze steadily. 'How is Freddie? How is she handling my being dead?'

'She's upset,' I said carefully. 'But she's coping.'

'Good. I liked her. It might have become more than that, but now I suppose I'll never know . . .'

'Concentrate on what's in front of you,' I said kindly. 'Help me out here, Arthur. Do you have any enemies?'

He looked at me pityingly. 'I'm a reporter. But I never wrote anything important enough for anyone to want me dead. I always hoped I would, but that's not going to happen now. All I have left is to find out who killed me. One last story to investigate, even if I'll never get to write it.'

'I could always find you a ghost writer,' I said.

Arthur glowered at me. 'Really not in the mood for humour, right now.'

'Oh, you'd be surprised at what's possible,' I said. 'Penny and I have a lot of experience when it comes to the stranger areas of the world.'

'I remember. Vampires and werewolves and psychics – oh, my. I always knew there was something weird about you two. What are you, exactly? Some kind of undercover agents?'

'Something like that,' I said.

'I knew it! Who do you work for? Would I have heard of them?'

I had to smile. 'Even dead, you're still thinking like a reporter.'

'Of course,' he said. 'When everything else has been taken from you, you can still cling to the truth.'

'The truth is the one thing that always matters,' I said.

'All right, then, give me the facts. Who are you, what are you, and what are you really doing here?'

'Sorry,' I said. 'I can't tell you any of that.'

'Why not?' said Arthur. 'I'm dead! Who am I going to tell?'

'I can hear you,' I said. 'So maybe others can, too.' I decided he needed distracting. 'How does it feel, being a ghost?'

He took a moment to think about it. 'I feel . . . surprisingly calm. I should be crying my eyes out, or raging at the heavens over the injustice of it all, but I'm not.'

'Probably just as well,' I said.

And then we both looked round as we heard people coming back down the hall. Going by their angry voices, it was a case of door one, hammer nil.

'I don't think I want to meet the others just yet,' said Arthur. 'I'm not ready for that.'

He disappeared. I blinked a few times and then swept my arm through the space where he'd been standing.

'I told you not to do that!' said Arthur's voice.

'You're still here?' I said.

'In spirit. But don't tell the others that I'm here.'

'Are you sure?' I said. 'I think it might help Freddie to know that you're still around.'

'Especially not her.' Arthur's voice was suddenly tired. 'I don't want her reminded of what we might have had. If the universe had been kinder. Look, you said it yourself. Someone in this group of ghost-botherers killed me. Let whoever it is think they got away with it, for the moment. If they relax, they might say something incriminating. That's how most murderers get caught, isn't it?'

'Usually,' I said. 'But there's not much usual about this case.' A thought struck me. 'Now that you're a ghost, can you see any other ghosts?'

'I haven't looked,' said Arthur's voice. 'And I don't think I want to. Just the idea gives me the creeps.'

'But you're dead! What have you got to be worried about?'

'I don't know! And I don't want to find out. Stick to solving my murder, Ishmael.'

'All right,' I said. 'How about this? I'll gather everyone together, and you appear before them. That might be enough to make someone confess.'

Arthur's voice sounded tempted. 'Yeah, I could point a finger and demand vengeance in a spooky voice . . . But I really don't think that would work. I have this feeling that none of them would be able to see me.'

'Lynn should be able to,' I said. 'Ghosts are her bread and butter.'

'Oh, please!' said Arthur. 'She's about as real as a six-pound note.'

His voice cut off as the others came storming in. Tom slammed the door shut behind them and threw his hammer into the open suitcase.

'Don't ask.'

'He hit the hinges with everything he had, and they didn't even notice,' said Freddie. 'Then he tried the lock, and the hammer bounced off and hit him on the head.'

'That door was built to keep things in, not out,' said Lynn.

'I even put my shoulder to it,' said Freddie. 'And there's not much can stand against that.' She rubbed her left shoulder and winced.

'Told you that wouldn't work,' said Lynn.

'Only after I tried,' said Freddie.

'I wanted to see how far you'd bounce,' said Lynn.

'I wonder how far I could make you bounce,' said Freddie.

'We'd need a chainsaw to get through that door,' Penny said quickly. 'And since none of us thought to bring one, I think we're all stuck here till the morning.'

'We could still try the upstairs windows,' said Tom.

'They're bound to be nailed shut as well,' said Freddie.

'You don't know that!' said Lynn.

'Want to bet on it?' said Freddie. 'Malcolm Welles put a lot of thought into making Harrow House his own private prison.'

Lynn nodded reluctantly. 'But he wouldn't have built a prison he couldn't get out of. There must be a way . . .'

'There was,' I said. 'He unlocked the front door and ran for it.'

'Then why didn't what was in here follow him out?' said Freddie.

'Perhaps it couldn't,' said Lynn. 'And that's why it's still here.'

'All we have to do is stay here till morning,' I said quickly. 'We'll be fine.'

'It is always possible that Arthur's death was just a coincidence,' Freddie said abruptly. 'A friend of mine died suddenly, a few years back, and when they opened him up, they found it was down to a weak artery in his brain. Could have popped any time, they said – like a time bomb in his head.' She stopped and looked at the floor where Arthur's body had been. 'Life isn't fair, and neither is death.'

'You were too old for him anyway,' said Lynn.

'Is that supposed to be comforting?' said Freddie.

I half expected Arthur to say something, but he didn't. I noticed Penny was looking at me oddly. I nodded for her to come and join me, away from the others.

'What?' I said quietly.

'What, yourself?' said Penny. 'I've never seen you so jumpy.'

'I've got a lot on my mind,' I said.

'Did you discover anything useful while we were gone?'

'Not as such, no.'

I didn't tell her about Arthur, because I didn't feel like telling anybody, just yet. Partly because I didn't want to spook anyone, but also because I didn't want to upset Arthur by revealing his presence before he was ready. And because I still wasn't ready to admit that he definitely was what he appeared to be. Or sometimes appeared to be.

Just thinking about him was enough to give me a headache.

Lynn and Freddie settled down in their chairs again, as far apart as they could get and still be in the same room. Lynn looked as if she was thinking hard, though I had no idea what about. Freddie also seemed lost in her own thoughts, most likely about Arthur. Tom was checking the readings on his screen, but it was obvious his heart wasn't in it. It was just something to do, to keep him occupied. I nodded to Penny to keep an eye on Lynn and Freddie, and went over to join Tom. He started speaking without even looking at me.

'Room temperature is back to normal. Everything is back in the normal range. But I don't know if that means anything. I don't think I can trust anything my instruments tell me, in this house.'

He sounded dejected. Science had let him down. One of the camera feeds slipped out of focus, and he made no move to adjust it.

'Don't you think it's important to keep track of what's happening in here?' I said.

'Not really.' He slapped the side of his screen, and the image sharpened again. 'I just want to survive till morning, so I can get the hell away from here and put this whole stupid mess behind me.' He sighed heavily. 'This kind of thing . . . It used to be all fun and games. Shining the harsh light of science into the dark corners of superstition . . . I never thought I'd have to watch someone die. I always thought I'd be good in a crisis, that I'd be right there trying to help . . . But when it all went to hell in a hurry, I just sat there and did nothing. I can't help thinking that if I hadn't let him down, Arthur might still be alive.'

'Don't think that for a moment,' I said. 'There was nothing you could have done. You're not responsible for what happened to him.'

Unless you are, I thought. *But I'm not sure you're that good an actor.*

Tom didn't say anything. He didn't care what I thought. He just kept on looking at his screen, as though still half hoping it might give him some answers he could live with. I moved away and left him to it.

I couldn't rule out Harrow House being involved in Arthur's death, especially given his surprise reappearance, but I wasn't prepared to accept anything in that line without some kind of evidence to back it up. Murder still seemed the most likely explanation, and the people in the circle with Arthur had to be the most likely suspects. Which meant I only had until help arrived in the morning to work out who did it, and how and why. Before the front door was opened and all my suspects scattered to the four winds.

Freddie suddenly sat up straight in her chair. 'Hey! Have any of you noticed that the scary atmosphere isn't here any more? I only just realized. Did anyone notice when it stopped?'

We all looked at each other, but no one had anything to offer.

'I think it disappeared after what happened to Arthur,' said Penny. 'It's hard to concentrate on a general bad feeling when someone has just died.'

'But where did it come from?' said Tom.

'This is a bad place,' said Lynn. 'It doesn't want us here.'

'All this time, I've been insisting that ghosts are just people,' Freddie said slowly. 'But now I think I was wrong. Ghosts are dead people. And that makes all the difference. All the things that make us human, the thoughts and emotions that shape us, come from the lives we've led. Take that away, and maybe a ghost could do anything, because it wouldn't care about anything.'

'There must be some humanity left in ghosts,' said Penny. 'Or why would they want to interact with the living at all?'

'Questions, questions,' Tom said irritably. 'And never an answer in sight. What I used to like about science was the idea that there were always answers to be found, if you just looked hard enough.'

'I don't care about ghosts any more,' said Lynn. 'Or this house. I just want to go home.'

'Well, you can't,' I said. 'So you might as well make yourself useful. You're the only psychic we've got, so are you picking up anything?'

Lynn looked at me. 'You've made it clear enough that you don't believe in my abilities. Why turn to me now?'

'I'm not as sure about some things as I used to be,' I said. 'Arthur's death has made me reassess how I see the world. Are you picking up anything, from anywhere in the house? Are we alone here?'

'I have no idea,' said Lynn. 'I'm not opening up my mind in this awful place. I don't trust it.'

'I don't think Harrow House cares what you want,' I said. I could feel Penny looking at me disapprovingly, wondering why I was pressuring Lynn, but I kept going. 'If you still want to be alive in the morning when help arrives, the best way to ensure that is to work out exactly what it is that's threatening us.'

'I don't know what's inhabiting this house!' Lynn said sharply. 'And I don't want to know. I was wrong to insist on the seance. Just attracting the house's attention was enough to get Arthur killed. The best thing we can do is stay quiet, keep our heads down and hope to hell that whatever's in here with us goes back to sleep.'

She turned around in her chair, curled up in a tight ball and refused to look at anyone. I caught Penny's eye, and we moved off a way.

'What was that all about?' Penny said quietly.

'Lynn has been acting strangely ever since Arthur died,' I said. 'Even if she is a compete fake, I would have expected her to be all over that, claiming to be in contact with Arthur's spirit so she could hit us with the usual comforting platitudes.'

'It's one thing to claim to be in contact with the dearly

departed and quite another to watch someone die right before your eyes,' said Penny. 'She's probably in shock.'

'She's keeping something from us,' I said. 'Though whether it has anything to do with Arthur's death remains to be seen. Did you overhear anything useful, down by the front door?'

'Tom was really quiet after he got hit in the head with his own hammer, Lynn became very sarcastic, and Freddie can swear like a soldier,' said Penny. 'Makes you wonder where she spends her evenings. So, Ishmael, are you ready to tell me what happened in this room while I was gone?'

I gave her my best innocent look. 'What makes you think something happened here?'

'Because I know you, Ishmael, and I can read you like a book, especially the dog-eared pages. You're so on edge you're halfway over it, and if I didn't know better, I'd swear you were suffering from shock, too.'

'All right,' I said. 'Something . . . unexpected did happen.'

I told her about Arthur, leaving nothing out and not sparing myself any embarrassment at being forced to change my position on the matter of ghosts. Penny looked at me wide-eyed until I'd finished, and then grinned broadly.

'I was right, and you were wrong . . . I am never going to let you forget that for as long as we both live. You met an actual ghost? That is so cool! What did Arthur look like? Was he transparent? Did he have a face like Lynn, only even paler? Does he know who killed him?'

'He looked perfectly normal,' I said. 'And no, he has no idea how he came to die so suddenly.'

'Hold everything, throw it in reverse,' said Penny. 'If he looked normal . . . how can you be sure it wasn't just him? Woken up from a coma, perhaps, and come wandering back in to find out what happened?'

'Because he appeared out of nowhere, right in front of me,' I said. 'And because I waved my hand back and forth through his body. He really didn't like that.'

'I wouldn't have either,' said Penny. 'Oh, I wish I'd been here to see him . . . It's not fair that you should be the one to have a close encounter with a ghost.'

'I am now far more open to the idea that Harrow House might actually be haunted,' I said.

'If only by Arthur.'

'Not just him,' I said. 'It's looking more and more likely that Malcolm Welles built this house specifically to imprison something, and that it might still be here, even after all these years.'

We both turned to look at the man scowling fiercely out of his portrait over the fireplace. He did look as if he knew something he wasn't planning on sharing with anyone else.

'I swear, if he winks at me, I will tear that portrait into pieces,' said Penny.

'This is a murder case,' I said sternly, 'not a Scooby Doo adventure.'

Penny sniffed loudly and gave me her own stern look. 'How could Arthur not know who killed him?'

'Because it all happened so quickly,' I said. 'It's not like someone clubbed him down with a blunt instrument.' I paused. 'I've never understood why those things are so popular. You can do much more damage with a sharp instrument.'

'Your mind goes wandering off on the strangest tangents sometimes,' said Penny.

'I think about these things.'

'I still can't believe Arthur appeared to you, and not me,' said Penny. 'Couldn't you at least get him to wait until I got back, so I could meet him as well?'

'He disappeared because he didn't want anyone else to see him,' I said.

'Can't you call him back?'

'He hasn't gone anywhere,' I said. 'He's still here, just invisible.'

Penny looked quickly around her, realized that wasn't going to work and fixed me with a hard stare.

'Why would he do that? Arthur never struck me as shy.'

'I think it's his way of coping with what's happened,' I said. 'Giving him some feeling of control over his new state of being. Or non-being, I suppose, if you want to be technical.'

'If he's still here, I want to talk to him,' said Penny. She lowered her voice. 'Arthur? Please show yourself. I promise I won't be frightened, or badger you with questions like Ishmael probably did.'

'You'd better do it,' I said to the empty air. 'She won't give either of us a moment's peace until you do.'

'It won't work,' said Arthur's voice, from just a little to one side. 'I just know you're the only one who can see and hear me.'

'Give it a try,' I said. 'Penny's really very sympathetic . . .'

'No rest for the recently and suddenly departed,' said Arthur's voice. 'What's the point of being dead if you can't enjoy a little peace and quiet?'

Penny looked at me accusingly. 'I'm only hearing one side of this conversation, aren't I?'

'Apparently,' I said. 'Can't you hear anything he's saying?'

'No,' said Penny, frowning. 'Tell him to materialize, Ishmael. Maybe I'll be able to hear him when I can see him.'

Arthur appeared out of nowhere, standing before us. Penny didn't react at all, still looking at the point where I'd been looking.

'Told you,' said Arthur.

'Is he here yet?' said Penny. 'I'm not seeing anything.'

Arthur thrust his face right into hers. 'Hello! Here I am! Dead man talking! What do I have to do to get your attention? Riverdance on the ceiling?'

Penny scowled and turned to me. 'I'm not feeling a chill, never mind a presence. I don't think he's really trying, Ishmael. You tell Arthur to get his act together, or I'll have Lynn exorcise him!'

She stalked off in a huff and threw herself into the nearest empty chair. The others looked at her, and then at me, decided we must have had a disagreement and went back to their own thoughts. None of them even glanced at where Arthur was standing. He made a rude gesture at the lot of them and then shrugged tiredly.

'I needn't have bothered with the invisible man bit. It seems I am only here for you, after all. Just as well. I wouldn't want Freddie to see me like this.'

'Why not?' I said. 'She's not the type to freak out at the

sight of a ghost, and it might give her some comfort to know for sure that there is life after death.'

'I'm not convinced there is,' said Arthur. 'I haven't seen any doors marked *Heaven* or *Hell*. No choirs of angels summoning me to my rest . . . For all I know, I could be nothing more than a last fading echo, the final glow of light before the candle goes out forever.'

'You're not the most optimistic of people, are you?'

'Do you blame me?'

'Then we'd better figure out why you're still here, while we can,' I said. 'And why you of all people should come back as a ghost.'

'Why shouldn't I?' said Arthur, bristling. 'I've as much right to come back as anyone else!'

'But that's just it,' I said. 'Most people don't come back. I've been around any number of sudden and violent deaths, and not one of them ever showed up afterwards to bother me.'

Arthur looked at me with new interest. 'You've seen lots of murder victims? That's amazing. Unless you're a serial killer. You're not, are you? If you are, you'd better stay the hell away from Freddie or I will haunt you wherever you go and never give you a moment's peace.'

'You're doing a pretty good job of that already,' I said. 'Relax, Arthur; I am not a serial killer.'

'Well, you would say that, wouldn't you?' Arthur said cunningly.

'Let us please try to concentrate on your murder,' I said. 'Why do you think you've returned?'

'I suppose it could be something to do with my family,' Arthur said slowly. 'We've always been closely tied to Harrow House, despite everything we've tried to do to rid ourselves of it.'

'But why am I the only one who can see and hear you? I don't know your family, and I'd never even heard of Harrow House before today.'

Arthur looked at me thoughtfully. 'There is something different about you . . . I can feel it in what used to be my bones. Like there's more to you than most people.'

He waited for me to say something, and when I didn't, he just shrugged.

'I don't suppose it's important. What matters is finding out who killed me. And since I can't question anyone, or search for clues, I think I'll just leave you to get on with it. I'm going home, to my family.'

'You think they'll be able to see you?'

'Even if they can't, I'll be able to see them,' said Arthur. 'And there are things I need to say, even if they can't hear me.'

He headed for the door. I did wonder for a moment whether the hall would be full of darkness again, once Arthur opened the door. But when he tried to turn the handle, his hand slipped right through it.

'All right!' he said harshly. 'If my hand can go through the handle, I'm going through the door. I am going home!'

Arthur walked straight at the door, only to slam up against it. He looked startled, and then very angry indeed. He picked a different spot and tried again, but the door wouldn't let him through. He turned his back on the door, with as much dignity as he could muster, and addressed me with a surprising amount of courtesy, considering both his hands had clenched into fists.

'Would you please be so kind as to open this door for me, Mr Jones?'

I went over to the door and opened it. And then I made a point of looking out into the brightly lit hall and listening ostentatiously, as though I thought I'd heard something. I needn't have bothered; when I glanced back, no one else was even looking in my direction. I stepped back from the door, and Arthur nodded curtly and strode past me. Only to crash to a sudden halt, as though he'd banged up against an invisible barrier. As though the door was still there, in spirit. He placed both hands against the air and pushed hard, but the empty doorway held firm. Arthur looked back at me.

'Always knew there was a good reason I hated mimes. All right, if the door won't cooperate . . .'

He tried walking through the wall next to the door, but didn't fare any better. After that, he lost his temper. He raged round the room, throwing himself at wall after wall, only to be bounced back each time. He even tried sticking his head through the glass of the nailed-up window, but was forced to retreat, defeated and swearing viciously.

Everyone else in the room was blind and deaf to the increasingly upset ghost in their midst. Lynn and Freddie were still sitting slumped in their separated chairs, Tom was still staring mournfully at his monitor screen, and Penny was going out of her way to look in every direction but mine. I closed the door and went to lean casually on the fireplace underneath the glowering portrait of Malcolm Welles. After a while, Arthur ran out of things to kick and swear at, and he stood in the middle of the room with his head hanging down. I think he would have been breathing hard – if he still breathed. He finally regained some of his self-control and came over to stand before me.

'What's going on, Ishmael?' he said quietly. 'Why can't I leave?'

'Something must be holding you here,' I said. 'I don't think Harrow House is finished with you yet.'

'Something?' said Arthur. 'What kind of something?'

'Whatever is still inhabiting the house, after all these years,' I said. 'Presumably it has some purpose in mind for you.'

'Like what?'

'Don't ask me,' I said. 'I'm new to this whole ghost business.'

'Join the club! We have T-shirts and secret handshakes.' And then Arthur stopped and looked around the room. 'How come no one's reacting to you apparently talking to yourself?'

'Because I am talking very quietly and barely moving my lips,' I said. 'Just one of the useful skills you pick up in the security business.'

Arthur scowled. 'Why do you think I'm being held here?'

'Perhaps because learning how and why you were killed will give us the answer to the mystery of Harrow House.'

'Typical,' said Arthur. 'Even as a ghost, I'm just a minor player in my own story. I think I'm going to disappear and sulk for a while.'

And he was gone.

'Are you still here, Arthur?' I said cautiously, but there was no response.

Freddie suddenly launched herself up out of her chair and strode over to stand before me. She glared at me challengingly, her fists planted on her hips.

'What are you up to, Jones? You've been behaving very strangely, ever since we got back.'

'I just can't help feeling that we're not alone here,' I said.

Freddie scowled. 'Wouldn't surprise me one bit. The nasty atmosphere may have done a bunk, but this house still doesn't feel right. I don't think it's finished playing with us yet.'

'You think someone else might die?'

'Don't you?' Freddie shook her head slowly. 'This house wants something from us.'

'Any idea what?'

'No,' said Freddie. 'Nothing that's happened so far makes any sense.' She softened a little and turned to look at the spot where the body had been. 'I can't believe Arthur is gone. We were just getting to know each other, and then he was taken from me . . .'

'Did you love him?' I said.

'No. But I might have. I think that's what hurts the most – losing all the things we might have meant to each other.'

Arthur appeared beside her. She just kept on looking at where his body used to be.

'How could you leave me, Arthur?'

'I didn't mean to,' he said. 'Freddie . . .'

He tried to take her hand in his, only to watch his hand ghost through hers. His mouth worked briefly, and then he disappeared again. Freddie pulled herself together and smiled brightly and only slightly artificially at me.

'I can't help feeling there's something different about you, Ishmael. Are you psychic?'

'No,' I said, careful not to smile. Because Freddie thought only in supernatural terms, the idea that I might not be as human as I appeared simply hadn't occurred to her. 'I am most definitely not psychic.'

'Of course he isn't psychic!' Lynn said loudly, from the depths of her chair. 'If he was, I'd know. I'm the only one with gifts here.'

And then we all looked round sharply, as scratching and

scrabbling sounds issued from inside the cabinet that held the stuffed animals. Everyone rose to their feet as the sounds grew louder and more definite, like sharp claws digging into the inside of the wooden doors. I could hear what sounded like the scuffling of small feet. And then the doors swung wide open, and one by one the stuffed animals turned their heads to look at us. Slow trickles of sawdust ran down from their mad glass eyes, like grey tears. Mouths opened wide with soft tearing sounds, and thin lips cracked as they pulled back to reveal sharp teeth.

'Lynn,' Freddie said quietly, 'what have you done?'

'This wasn't me,' said Lynn, staring numbly at the stuffed animals. 'This is nothing to do with me.'

'You're the one who called out to the house to answer you,' said Freddie.

And then she broke off as the stuffed animals started talking in rough, harsh voices. Horrible sounds that grated on the nerves, from unliving objects forced to take on the attributes of life.

'Why won't you listen?' said a fox.

'You must listen,' said an owl.

'There's something in the walls,' said a squirrel.

I stepped forward, and all the stuffed heads turned jerkily to look at me. Their gaze was horribly empty, but I had no doubt they could see me.

'Who's speaking?' I said. 'Is this the house or something in the house?'

'You know us,' said the squirrel. 'And we know you. Why won't you listen?'

'What do you want?' I said.

The squirrel's mouth opened even wider, as though trying to force words out, but the jaw suddenly broke and dropped open, hanging uselessly. The squirrel reached up with its small stubby arms and clawed deep furrows in its face. And then all the animals turned on each other, biting and clawing in a horrid frustrated rage. Sawdust streamed from gaping wounds. Until finally, one by one, the animals fell still . . . as though they'd exhausted themselves in trying to talk to us.

I slowly approached the open cabinet and prodded a few of

the torn and savaged bodies with a cautious finger, but none of them moved. They were just badly stuffed objects again. I carefully closed the cabinet's doors.

'What the hell was that all about?' said Penny.

'It's the house,' said Freddie.

'But nothing they said made any sense,' said Tom. 'Why make such an effort to talk to us, just to speak gibberish?'

Freddie frowned hard. 'The squirrel said, "There's something in the walls." You said the same thing earlier, Lynn.'

'Did I?' Lynn seemed honestly surprised. 'I don't remember that. I have no idea what it might mean.'

'Are you sure?' said Freddie. 'Think, Lynn!'

'I am thinking! And don't shout at me!'

'If the house is so keen to communicate with us,' said Tom, 'why use stuffed animals?'

'Maybe the house is insane,' said Penny.

Nobody liked the sound of that. I cleared my throat, to draw everyone's attention back to me.

'Perhaps this mention of a secret hidden in the walls is a clue to where the treasure is?'

'There's treasure in this house?' said Tom, trying hard to sound only scientifically interested.

'Could be,' said Freddie. 'Ghosts and treasure often go together.'

'You would think that,' said Lynn.

'Hush, child,' said Freddie. 'Adults are talking.'

'Are we supposed to break the walls open?' said Penny.

'I've got some really big hammers,' said Tom.

'What treasure are we talking about?' said Lynn.

'The lost fortune of the Welles family,' Tom said impatiently. 'It's in all the books. *Something in the walls* . . . Could the animals have meant somewhere in here?' He moved over to the nearest wall and tapped it here and there, but there wasn't even a suggestion of a hollow sound. Tom scowled, thinking. 'Maybe there's a clue somewhere inside one of the walls as to where we should look for the treasure?'

'And maybe that's not it at all,' said Freddie. 'Does anything about our experiences suggest this house has our best interests in mind? We can't trust anything it says. It killed Arthur.'

We all stopped talking out of respect for her loss, and that was when we heard new soft scratching sounds.

'Now what?' said Freddie.

We looked around the room, searching for the source of the quiet noises. In the end, Penny pointed with a perfectly steady hand at a tall standing mirror. Dark figures were moving inside the glass, drifting this way and that as though caught in some deep underwater tide. Now and then one of them would reach out to touch the inside of the glass, making the soft scratching sounds. We moved over to stand before the mirror, and once we were all in place, the figures suddenly snapped into sharp focus, as our reflections. All the faces in the mirror were horribly distorted, as though our reflections had suffered terrible experiences. Arthur's reflection was there too, snarling back at us. I glanced behind me, to see if his ghost had joined us, but there was no sign of him.

'Is everyone seeing this?' said Tom.

'Of course we see it!' said Lynn.

'Then what does it mean?' said Tom.

'It means the house isn't finished with us,' said Freddie.

Our reflections crowded together, pressing up against the other side of the mirror. Their hands scrabbled against the glass, and then they beat on it with their fists, as though the mirror was a window into our world, and they wanted out. As though they were determined to get to us – whatever it took.

'Why are they doing this?' said Penny.

'Perhaps they want to pull us through the mirror,' said Lynn. 'So they can take our place here.'

'Is this real?' said Tom. 'I mean, really real?'

'I don't know!' said Freddie. 'Why is Arthur there?'

And all the time our reflections were desperately trying to speak, to tell us something important, but not a sound reached us from the other side of the mirror. I stepped forward, standing directly in front of the glass, and immediately all the reflections fixed their gaze on me.

'What is it?' I said. 'What are you trying to tell us?'

'You sure you want to know?' said Tom.

'Yes!' I said. 'This has to mean something!'

My reflection suddenly lashed out with his fist, and the inside of the glass cracked. And just like that, our reflections were normal again. Just five people staring at themselves, and no sign anywhere of Arthur. We all backed slowly away from the mirror, not wanting to take our eyes off it, but it stayed just a mirror.

'I'm getting really tired of all these spooky parlour tricks,' said Freddie.

'The house is trying to communicate with us,' I said.

'What could it have to say to us that we would want to hear?' said Tom. 'Think of everything it's done so far!'

'I'm tired,' said Lynn. 'I don't want to think about this any more.'

She went back to curl up in her chair again, like a small child who'd stayed up past her bedtime.

Tom shook his head, one fist banging frustratedly against his hip.

'None of this makes any sense!' he said loudly. 'Maybe the house really is crazy, and we're all trapped inside the mind of a mad thing.'

He went back to his screen, where at least he could feel as if he was in control of something.

'I want to know why Arthur was in the mirror!' Freddie insisted.

'Maybe because he's still with us, in spirit,' I said.

She rounded on me angrily, and then stopped herself and went back to sit in her chair and stare at nothing. Penny came over to join me.

'Sorry about the little outburst earlier,' she said.

'What outburst?' I said, and we shared a smile.

'I don't like losing my temper,' said Penny. 'It never solves anything, and it always makes me feel bad afterwards. Maybe something really is getting inside our heads and messing with our thinking.'

'Wouldn't surprise me,' I said.

'You did see Arthur's ghost, didn't you? And talk with him?'

'Yes,' I said. 'I think I'd be happier if I could dismiss him as an hallucination, but when stuffed animals start talking, and our own reflections try to break out of the mirror, ghosts don't even register in the weird happenings stakes. And if Arthur was murdered, we need to find out who did it, to help him move on. Why are you smiling?'

'Just when I think you can't surprise me any more . . . You won't let anyone down, will you? Even when they're dead. Are you still convinced Arthur's killer is someone in this room?'

'I haven't seen the house do anything yet that I would call actually threatening,' I said. 'But people can always be dangerous. And since there's no evidence anyone broke into the house before we arrived, the killer has to be someone in this room.'

'Any motives you feel like mentioning?' said Penny.

'Arthur said he was going to expose Lynn as a fraud,' I said thoughtfully. 'And it's always possible that Freddie wanted something from Arthur that he was unwilling to give. Hell hath no fury . . .'

'What about Tom?'

'We were all right there when Arthur died, but no one saw anything because we were too busy concentrating on the darkness in the door,' I said. 'Maybe someone arranged for that to happen. And which of us knows enough about science and technology to arrange something like that?'

We both looked at Tom, sitting cross-legged on the floor before the screen, his laptop balanced across his knees. His fingers moved slowly across the keyboard, with no obvious purpose.

'And yet no one touched Arthur,' Penny said firmly. 'We all saw that in the recording. No one was even looking in his direction when he died.'

'We must be missing something,' I said.

'Maybe that's why Arthur came back,' said Penny. 'Because we weren't getting anywhere.'

'Then why am I the only one who can see and hear him?'

'I don't know,' said Penny. 'Because you're . . . not from around here?'

'Then why have I never seen a ghost before?' I said. 'After all the sudden deaths I've been involved with, I should be hip deep in the things by now.'

'Perhaps because death doesn't mean the same thing to you as it does to us,' Penny said slowly. 'To us mere humans.'

'Penny . . .' I said carefully. 'Let's not get caught up in that again.'

'I have to,' said Penny. 'Because you're not listening. It's because humans know we only have three score years and ten that our lives have shape and purpose. We're driven to get things done, because we know we won't have enough time to do everything that needs doing. But you don't have that problem. You can always take the long view because you have all the time in the world.'

'I don't know that,' I said. 'I could die tomorrow, from accident or malice, just like everyone else.'

'And yet you don't,' said Penny. 'You just keep going. You haven't aged a day in more than fifty years . . . Can you die? Does death mean the same thing to you, to your other self, as it does to a human? I'm going to grow old and die, and when I do, you'll just move on and forget me.'

'I would never do that!'

'You know that's not true!' Penny met my gaze fiercely. 'You've walked out on people before, because you thought they were a threat to your secret existence, or just because they were getting too close. You don't know how to be close to anyone. Maybe I need to walk away from you, if only for my pride's sake. I won't be an old woman clinging to a young man's arm and wondering why he's still there.'

'Penny . . .'

'Don't,' she said. 'There's a reason why all the old myths agree that mortals should never love immortals. Because it isn't fair on either of them. Whatever happens in this house, whatever the truth turns out to be, we're done, Ishmael. It's over. For both our sakes.'

She walked away from me, and didn't look back once.

FIVE

Things Seen and Unseen

I didn't go after Penny. I couldn't – not until I had some kind of answers to the questions she'd raised. The only thing I was sure of was that I had no intention of letting her walk out of my life. Because she was my life, in every way that mattered.

On top of all that, I still had a murder to solve. It had been a long time since I'd had to work a mystery on my own. I'd grown used to having Penny at my side, as a sounding board for my ideas and to point out the subtler areas of human interaction I still sometimes had problems with. I couldn't ask any of my potential suspects, so that meant there was only one person left I could turn to.

'Arthur?' I said quietly. 'Are you still hanging around? Because I could really use your help.'

He appeared beside me, shaking his head disbelievingly. 'You don't just need help; you need a whole couchful of relationship counsellors on speed dial.'

I looked at him accusingly. 'You were eavesdropping.'

He shrugged, not looking even a little bit guilty. 'What else is there to do around here? If you don't want sympathy, which I've never been much good at anyway, what do you want?'

'I need you to help me solve your murder.'

He looked at me blankly. 'Why are you asking me? I already told you I didn't see who did it.'

'Because,' I said patiently, 'you're the only person in this room I can be sure didn't do it.'

He nodded slowly. 'OK, that makes sense . . . I suppose.'

'Be my partner,' I said. 'And help me drop the hammer on whoever did this to you.'

'Oh, I am in!' said Arthur. 'What can I do?'

'I don't know,' I said. 'What *can* you do?'

Arthur took a moment to think about it. 'Well . . . it seems

I can't leave this room, so I can't go looking for clues. And I can't interrogate people or intimidate them, so I'll have to leave that to you. I can see people's auras, which I couldn't before. Didn't even know people had auras . . .'

'What use is that?'

'I can tell from changes in the aura whether people are lying, or being evasive, or hiding something,' said Arthur. 'The colours change and . . . Look, just take my word for it, OK? Of course, one of the first things you learn as a journalist is that most people lie like they breathe, and for any number of reasons. Sometimes I think they just do it to stay in practice.'

I had to ask. 'Do I have an aura?'

'Of course.'

'What's it like?'

He considered me carefully. 'Lots of purple.'

I decided I wasn't going to touch that one. 'OK . . . I will ask people pertinent and probing questions, and you can tell me how much I should trust their answers.'

'So you're leaving it to me to do all the heavy lifting?' said Arthur.

'You want to find out who killed you, don't you?'

'Oh, great! Hit me over the head with emotional blackmail, why don't you?' And then Arthur broke off and looked at me narrowly. 'Why are you so determined to find my killer? It's not like we're close or anything.'

'Because this is what I do,' I said steadily. 'And because it's the right thing to do.'

Arthur smiled briefly. 'I don't often get to hear that, in my line of work. It does make a nice change.'

'You didn't deserve what happened to you,' I said. 'So with your assistance, I will do my best to see you get some kind of justice. Maybe . . . that's what you're here for.'

Arthur thrust out a hand for me to shake, and then he remembered and took it back. I turned away, so he could have a moment to himself, and raised my voice to address the room.

'Could I have everyone's attention, please?'

'If you want to excuse yourself, just go ahead and do it,' said Freddie. 'You don't need to raise your hand and ask permission. Though I don't know where you think you're going to go. I haven't seen a toilet anywhere.'

'Must be upstairs,' said Tom.

Lynn smiled sweetly at me. 'Good luck with the rotting floorboards. And you'd better be careful with your aim, if you don't want to make things even worse.' And then she stopped and frowned. 'Oh, hell . . . I didn't need to go at all until you raised the subject, but now I can't stop thinking about it. How much longer will it be, until people start arriving in the morning?'

'Hours,' said Tom, grinning maliciously. 'Hours and hours.'

'Oh, hell,' said Lynn, crossing her legs.

'I don't need to use the toilet,' I said.

'Well, then, good for you,' said Freddie. 'But you're not the only one here.'

'I am convinced that Arthur didn't just die,' I said, refusing to be diverted from what mattered.

Everyone looked at the spot where Arthur's body had been. I couldn't read anything in their faces. One by one they turned back to me – apart from Penny, who continued to stare at the patch of floor so she wouldn't have to look at me.

'Well, of course Arthur didn't just die,' Lynn said finally. 'The house killed him. And it could still do the same to us if we don't find some way out of here.'

'Will you stop going on about that?' said Freddie. 'There isn't any other way out!'

'We don't know that for sure,' said Tom.

'Where else is there to look?' said Freddie.

'I don't like being here!' said Lynn. She was sounding more and more childlike. 'I should never have come to this horrible place. It isn't at all like I thought it was going to be. I want to go home.'

'Will you please calm the hell down!' said Freddie. 'It isn't that bad. Not right now. At least the appalling atmosphere hasn't come back. That has to mean something.'

'Yes,' said Tom. 'But what?'

'I don't know!' said Freddie. 'You're the scientist!'

'And a lot of help that's been,' said Lynn.

'If I could just drag you all back to the subject at hand,' I said. 'It's my belief Arthur was murdered. By someone in this room.'

Lynn, Tom and Freddie all looked honestly shocked, as though the thought had never struck home before. And then everyone looked suspiciously at everyone else, before finally turning back to look at me.

'As if we didn't have enough on our minds,' said Tom, 'now we have to worry about whether one of us is a murderer?'

Freddie leaned forward in her chair, to better fix me with a cold glare. 'What makes you so sure Arthur was killed? I saw him close up when we carried him out, and there wasn't a mark on him.'

'It couldn't have been murder,' said Lynn. 'I mean, it just couldn't! We were all right here with him when it happened. We would have seen something.'

'Would we?' said Tom. 'We were all concentrating on the door, trying to make out whatever was hiding in the darkness.'

'We still have no idea what that darkness was,' said Freddie. 'Or why it hasn't returned.'

'Do you want it to come back?' said Lynn. 'The last time it was here, somebody died.'

There was an uncomfortable silence, as they all considered the implications of that. I took advantage of the pause to glance meaningfully at Arthur.

'Lynn is definitely hiding something,' he said immediately. 'So are Tom, Freddie and your ex-girlfriend. Perfectly normal human behaviour, in other words.'

'You can leave Penny out of it,' I said. 'I know what's on her mind.'

'She could still be a suspect,' said Arthur.

'No, she couldn't,' I said firmly.

He shrugged. 'Have it your own way. I'm just saying . . .'

'Is there anything about Freddie that catches your eye?' I said.

'Her aura is all over the place,' Arthur said slowly. 'But that could just be down to her feeling upset. Why do you ask?'

'Because she doesn't seem nearly upset enough over your death.'

Arthur shook his head firmly. 'It's just her way. I really don't see Freddie as my killer.'

'Why not?' I said. 'Just because she was trying to seduce you?'

He grinned. 'You say that like it's a bad thing. And anyway, she cared about me. She really did. I could tell.'

'But what if she didn't?' I said. 'What if everything she said and did was nothing more than a smokescreen, so she could get close enough to kill you?'

'I'd hate to have a mind like yours,' said Arthur. 'Why would Freddie want to do something like that?'

'I don't know,' I said. 'That's why I'm asking questions.'

I realized everyone was staring at me. I met their gaze steadily.

'What?'

'Why are you muttering to yourself?' said Tom.

'Yes,' said Freddie. 'Cut it out. It's getting on my nerves.'

'You're weird, Ishmael,' said Lynn.

'It's just something he does,' said Penny. 'He says it helps him think.'

I shot her a grateful look, but she had already turned away.

'Why would one of us want to kill Arthur?' Lynn said stubbornly. 'What reason could we possibly have? It's not like he was anyone important.'

'I could have been!' Arthur said loudly. 'You don't know! And even on the worst day I ever had, I was still more important than some sanctimonious low-rent mind-reading act, telling people what they want to hear in return for cash in hand and your face in the paper!'

'Ten out of ten for moral outrage, Arthur, but try to keep the noise down,' I said quietly. 'I'm trying to run an interrogation here.'

'They can't hear me!'

'I can.'

He sniffed and folded his arms sulkily. 'Well, get on with it, then.'

I went back to listening to the others.

'Arthur might not have been particularly diplomatic,' said

Freddie, 'but he hadn't known any of us long enough to make that kind of enemy.'

'It's not like we know much about him,' Tom said dubiously. 'In fact, we don't know that much about any of us. We could have brought all kinds of past history and emotional baggage with us. For all we know, anyone in this room could have it in them to be a killer.'

Lynn sat up in her chair and looked quickly round the room, like a frightened child who'd suddenly realized she was surrounded by adults she couldn't trust.

'Even if someone here did kill Arthur,' she said tremulously, 'it might not be their fault.'

'OK . . .' said Freddie. 'This should be interesting. What makes you think that, Lynn?'

'We know that something bad happened here, long ago,' Lynn said slowly. 'Bad enough to poison the spiritual wells of Harrow House. It's still here, seeping out into the atmosphere. It could be that the house has been subtly influencing us all along, to do things we would never normally dream of doing.'

'You sound like you're trying to establish a case for someone's defence,' Tom said dryly.

'We haven't felt the bad atmosphere for ages,' said Freddie.

'Perhaps because the house has already achieved what it wanted,' said Lynn. 'To put its thoughts inside one of us, so that person would have no choice but to kill whoever the house wanted dead.'

'But if that was true, it would mean we couldn't trust anyone,' said Tom. 'Because any one of us might not be who we thought we were.'

'If one of us had been driven out of our mind, we'd hardly be sitting here talking rationally about it, would we?' Freddie said sharply.

'Perhaps now the madness has passed, the killer is lying low,' said Lynn, 'hoping to avoid drawing attention to themselves.'

'You're the psychic,' I said. 'Shouldn't you be able to tell if one of us has been got at?'

She glared at me. 'My powers don't work that way.'

'So you say,' said Tom.

'I have a feeling for places and settings,' Lynn said coldly. 'But I have no way of telling what's going on inside your heads. If I did, I might not feel so frightened all the time.' She slumped back in her chair, looking suddenly even smaller. 'I hate being here, and I hate all of this. I'm so tired . . . I just want to go to sleep and not wake up till it's over. But I'm too scared to sleep.'

Tom turned to Freddie, but she was already shaking her head.

'My skill sets are all to do with the powers of nature . . . though I like to think I would have noticed an actual possession taking place right in front of me.' She looked at each of us in turn, frowning thoughtfully. 'I can offer you this much: I'm not feeling any unnatural presence in this room. At the moment.'

'And all my instruments are sleeping on the job,' said Tom. 'Whatever's going on here, they can't cope with it.'

'I'd like to know why the house keeps showing us these sudden flashes of power and high strangeness, and then goes quiet,' I said.

'Perhaps it only has so much energy to draw on,' said Lynn. 'It drains itself showing us things, like the darkness and the stuffed animals and the mirror . . . and then it has to rest and recover before it can try again.' She rubbed awkwardly at her forehead, as though troubled by a sudden pain. 'Sometimes, I think this house is alive . . .'

'Try to get some sleep,' said Freddie, not unkindly.

I looked to Tom. 'Could any of your equipment detect an energy surge like that?'

He looked at his screen. 'It would depend on what kind of energy was involved. Most of this was only ever designed to deal with the kind of events you'd expect in traditional hauntings. But I don't think there's anything traditional about Harrow House.'

'I wonder . . .' said Freddie.

'What?' Lynn said tiredly, not even looking at her. 'What do you wonder?'

'Whether this house is running experiments on us,' said Freddie. 'Putting us through hoops, just to watch us jump.'

'Stop it!' said Lynn. 'That's a horrible idea! I don't even want to think about that.'

Freddie shook her head. 'How did you ever get to be a celebrated psychic, with such delicate sensibilities?'

Lynn looked at her coldly. 'You think this was something I chose? I do it because I'm good at it.'

'Good at parting suckers from their money,' said Arthur.

'Did you ever find any hard evidence to support that?' I said quietly.

'Some,' said Arthur. 'And I had contacts who swore they could get me more. I was putting a major story together. Real front-page stuff. Now all I can do is hope someone at the *Herald* will be able to make enough sense out of my notes to stick it to her properly.'

'Hush,' I said.

'If the killer knows they're under suspicion, what's to stop them killing again?' Tom said slowly. 'They might feel they have no choice but to murder everyone here, rather than risk us telling what we know to the authorities.'

'But what could we tell them?' said Lynn. 'We don't know anything.'

'Finally!' said Freddie. 'Something we can agree on.'

They were all studying each other warily. Lynn looked as though she wanted to hide behind something, Tom looked as if he was thinking of making a run for the door, and Freddie looked ready to punch out anyone who got too close. Penny watched all of them in turn, but said nothing.

'They're all scared,' Arthur said quietly. 'And I mean *really* scared. But I don't think they're scared of the same things.'

'How do you mean?' I said.

'I'm not sure,' said Arthur. 'It's hard to interpret what I'm seeing, but their auras are flaring and buzzing like they're going to explode.'

'Can you tell if any of them are keeping something important from the rest of us?'

'They're all concealing something!' said Arthur. 'Very definitely including your ex. Her aura shows whole extra levels of shielding . . . As though she's trained herself to not even think about certain things.'

'I told you to leave her out of this.'

'It's to do with you, isn't it?' said Arthur. He looked at me searchingly. 'Something to do with your being security, or maybe to do with one of your past cases? No, that's not it. Whatever it is she's hiding, it's definitely to do with you. I always knew there was something off about you, Ishmael. What is it? What am I missing?'

'Concentrate on the murder suspects,' I said calmly.

'I think we should just stay here and watch each other till morning, and then let the authorities sort it all out,' said Freddie.

Lynn laughed harshly. 'Do you really think the police are going to believe anything we have to say about what we've witnessed here?'

'All we could tell them for certain is that Arthur collapsed suddenly and died,' I said. 'For no obvious reason.'

'Exactly,' said Lynn. 'We don't have any real evidence that it might be murder.'

'Or that the house turned anyone into a killer,' said Freddie.

Lynn turned on her. 'Is it any easier to believe that someone came here intending to kill Arthur?'

'If we are stuck in this house with a murderer,' Tom said slowly, 'we have to figure out who it is, so we can lock them up somewhere. It's the only way we can feel safe.'

'But what if there isn't any way to tell?' said Lynn. 'What good does all this talking do, when there's nothing we can depend on to make sense?'

'We should be safe enough, as long as we all stick together,' said Penny.

'Damn right,' Freddie said immediately. 'You won't catch me going off on my own. I watch horror movies. It's always the ones who separate themselves from the pack that end up leaving the film early – often in strange and inventive ways.'

'But what if we have to . . . "go"?' said Lynn. 'I'm starting to wish I hadn't drunk the herbal tea.'

'I have a couple of water bottles in one of my cases,' Tom said diffidently. 'I could always empty them out . . .'

'Not very practical where us girls are concerned,' said Freddie. 'Unless you've got a funnel in there as well.'

'I think I saw a vase in one of the other rooms,' said Tom.

'Could we please change the subject?' said Lynn.

'You started it,' said Freddie.

'And I really wish I hadn't,' said Lynn.

'It's all in the mind,' said Penny.

'No, it isn't – it's all in the bladder!' said Lynn, crossing her legs tightly.

'Tell them they can piss in the fireplace,' said Arthur. 'I don't mind, and Malcolm deserves it. The others can always turn their backs and whistle, if someone's feeling a bit bashful.'

'Really not helping, Arthur,' I said.

'The house knows we're talking about it,' Lynn said suddenly. 'I'm feeling a presence, right here in the room with us, listening to everything we say.'

'Will you stop saying things like that!' said Tom. 'Feelings aren't evidence!'

'They can be, in our line of work,' said Freddie.

'Oh, please,' said Tom. 'Don't confuse my ghost-hunting skills with your mystic bullshit. I deal strictly in science.'

'Right up to the point where it fails you,' said Freddie.

'Science hasn't failed me!' said Tom.

'Then how do you explain all the weird stuff that's happened?' said Freddie. 'The dark in the door, the stuffed animals that talked, the things in the mirror?'

'It is possible that there are strong electromagnetic fields at work in this house,' Tom said steadily. 'Powerful enough to affect our minds and make us see things.' He looked at the cabinet, with its closed doors. 'What if . . . none of that actually happened? What if it was all just in our minds?'

We all turned around to stare at the cabinet.

'You mean, what we experienced was just a shared hallucination?' said Lynn. 'Is that even possible?'

'It's got to be more likely than a bunch of stuffed animals talking nonsense and then ripping the sawdust out of each other,' said Tom.

'All right,' said Freddie. 'If you're so convinced, you go and open the cabinet doors and take a look. Show us what's in there.'

'Don't do it, Tom,' Lynn said quickly. 'You can't trust anything in this house.'

'I'll do it,' I said. 'This is one of the few things we can check for ourselves. If the stuffed animals aren't actually damaged . . .'

'But if the house has been making us see things, how can we trust anything we see?' said Lynn.

'Everything seems quiet for the moment,' said Freddie. 'If the house is busy recharging its batteries, I say let's take advantage of it.'

I looked at Penny, and for the first time she met my gaze and nodded slightly. I walked steadily over to the cabinet and reached for the handles.

'Be careful, Ishmael!' Lynn said suddenly. 'Don't let them get out!'

I glanced back at her. 'I think I can handle a few stuffed animals, even if they are still in a bad mood.'

'They could bite!' said Lynn.

'They could try,' I said. 'But even then, it's not like they're going to give me rabies, is it?'

I pulled the doors open and stepped back, so everyone could get a good view. All the shelves were empty. There wasn't a single badly stuffed creature to be seen anywhere in the cabinet, and nothing to suggest they'd ever been there.

'They can't just have disappeared!' said Freddie.

'Unless they were never there,' I said.

'Maybe they were the ghosts of dead animals,' said Lynn.

'Ghosts don't get themselves stuffed,' said Freddie.

'They only ever existed inside our minds,' said Tom. 'Just another trick the house has played on us.'

'Or another attempt to communicate with us,' said Penny. 'Like the voice on your phone.'

I closed the cabinet doors. 'Tom, could you pull up the recording of us talking with the stuffed animals, so we can watch what really happened?'

'Yes!' Tom said immediately, pleased at having a straightforward problem to deal with. 'I can do that! And my cameras don't lie.'

He settled down before his screen, grabbed his laptop and searched for the right sequence. The live camera feeds disappeared from the screen as everyone came over to join him. Even Arthur drifted in behind me, so he could peer over my shoulder. The recording showed our previous selves confronting a completely empty cabinet. We all appeared seriously spooked, but the only voices on the soundtrack were our own.

'Show us the mirror sequence,' said Freddie.

Tom put that on the screen, and we all watched ourselves stare in horror at perfectly normal reflections.

'How could we have been fooled so completely?' said Penny.

'It's the house,' said Lynn. 'We see what it wants us to see.'

'All because it wants to talk to us?' said Freddie, frowning. 'What does it have to say that could be so important? And why does it keep doing it the hard way?'

'Perhaps because there isn't an easy way,' I said. 'Tom, show us the door full of darkness, please.'

We watched ourselves stare open-mouthed at a doorway full of perfectly normal hall light. Tom shut down the recording before we got to Arthur's death, without having to be told, and we all looked at each other.

'If the dark was a purely supernatural experience,' Lynn said finally, 'it might not show up on a recording.'

'If you can't record it, it didn't really happen,' said Tom.

'You're not listening to me!' said Lynn. 'This house can put things in our heads. The experience is real, even if what we see isn't!'

'OK . . .' said Penny. 'That is a seriously creepy thought. Even more than a house full of ghosts.'

'Tom?' I said. 'You are frowning so hard you'll break something in a minute. What's wrong?'

'If there were any serious electromagnetic fields operating in this house, powerful enough to affect the human brain, I'd expect my sensors to have picked them up,' Tom said slowly. 'And my readings aren't showing anything like that. I suppose it could be some unknown form of energy . . .'

'You mean magic?' said Lynn.

Tom looked at her.

'How does any of this help decide which one of us killed Arthur?' Freddie said doggedly.

'If the house has been messing with our senses, who knows what evidence we might have missed?' said Tom.

'We were all holding hands when Arthur died,' Lynn said stubbornly. 'I don't see how we could be fooled about something as basic as that.'

'We could, if that was what the house wanted,' said Freddie.

'Then how can we be sure Arthur really is dead?' Tom said suddenly.

There was a sudden flare of hope in Freddie's eyes, but it died just as quickly.

'No,' she said. 'I felt his dead weight in my hands when I carried him out. I had to turn my face away from the smell of his death.'

'I am so sorry, Freddie,' Arthur said quietly. 'You should never have had to go through something like that.'

'Arthur was murdered,' Freddie said flatly. 'Either by something in this house or by one of us.'

'If anyone had done anything to Arthur, we would have seen it on the recording,' said Tom.

'Not if the killer was really good at sleight of hand,' I said. 'What if someone jabbed him surreptitiously with a needle? We wouldn't have spotted that.'

'We were all holding hands!' Lynn said loudly. 'You all saw it on the recording! Nobody let go until he fell backwards, already dying! Arthur couldn't have been killed by one of us, because none of us could possibly have done it.'

'Just because you don't want something to be true doesn't mean it can't be,' said Freddie. 'And there is one very suspicious person in this room . . . Ishmael Jones!'

'And the girl!' said Tom.

'What?' Penny said dangerously. 'Tell me you did not just refer to me as "the girl"! I am Ishmael's partner! Or, at least, I was. It's complicated.'

'We don't know anything for certain about you or Ishmael,' Freddie said accusingly. 'Everyone else has a clear and obvious reason to be here. We all have established reputations in our chosen fields – as a psychic, a local historian, a ghost-chaser. But you two just turned up out of nowhere claiming to be *security*, whatever that means. You claim to be representing the buyer of this house, but you haven't offered any evidence to back that up. Do you honestly expect us to just take your word for it? You could be anybody!'

Lynn and Tom moved quickly to stand with Freddie. To show their support, or because there's safety in numbers. They all stared challengingly at me and Penny. I stared calmly back.

'I'm the only one who seems convinced there is a killer,' I said.

'What better way to divert our suspicions?' said Freddie.

'I always knew there was something strange about you, Ishmael,' said Lynn.

'Maybe they're really here for the treasure,' said Tom.

'Or they're in league with whatever's in the house,' said Freddie. 'None of the weird stuff started happening until they turned up.'

'If we had come here intending to kill Arthur,' I said patiently, 'we wouldn't have done it in front of a whole crowd of witnesses, would we?'

'Murderers really don't like to stand out and be noticed,' said Penny. 'In our experience.'

'Whatever that is,' Freddie said darkly.

'If you don't have anything to hide, why don't you tell us what you and Ishmael were quarrelling about?' said Tom. 'Why you suddenly stopped talking to each other?'

'I forgot her birthday,' I said.

'Even after I reminded him,' said Penny, not missing a beat.

'Ah,' said Tom. 'Yes . . . that would do it.'

'You believe them?' said Freddie.

Tom shrugged helplessly. 'They're not acting like killers.'

'Killers rarely do,' said Freddie. 'In my experience.'

'Which is?' I said politely.

'Far too much television, probably,' said Lynn.

'I watch a lot of cop shows,' said Tom. 'For a murder, they always say you need to establish motive, means and opportunity. So, let's start with motive. Which one of us could have had a reason to want Arthur dead?'

'He was very irritating,' said Lynn.

'He was a reporter,' said Freddie.

'But none of us had even met Arthur before tonight,' said Lynn. 'Unless someone has been keeping it to themselves . . .'

There was a general shaking of heads.

'I think Arthur would have mentioned that,' said Tom.

'And he was very emphatic that he only came here because his editor insisted,' said Penny.

'We all have our own reasons for being here,' said Lynn.

'Very different reasons,' said Tom.

'The only thing we all have in common is Harrow House,' said Freddie.

'Not just the house,' said Tom. 'We're all fascinated by the mystery of why so many strange things have happened here. Arthur said he'd done a lot of research on the subject; perhaps he uncovered something that someone else didn't want revealed.'

'Oh, he's good,' said Arthur.

'What if he did?' said Lynn. 'There have been any number of books written about the strange history of Harrow House. And a television documentary. What could Arthur have dug up that everyone else missed?'

'Perhaps something only his family knew, which they didn't want made public,' said Tom. 'Things they were ready to tell him that they could never reveal to anyone else. What if someone in his family was worried we might uncover something that would damage their reputation?'

'This is such bullshit,' said Arthur. 'My family doesn't know anything, because they don't want to know anything. And we haven't had a reputation worth speaking of in generations.'

'Hush,' I said.

'Stop telling me to hush! I'm supposed to be your partner!'

'Then be helpful, and hush,' I said.

'I'm going off you.'

'Arthur could have been sent here with instructions to protect his family's reputation at all costs,' said Tom.

'What reputation?' said Freddie. 'Everyone knows old Malcolm Welles was a monster. Or kept a monster in his cellar. Or something like that.'

'I'm not sure where this is going,' said Penny. 'Are you

suggesting Arthur had a reason to kill one of us, and that the murderer acted out of self-defence?'

'It doesn't sound very likely, does it?' said Tom.

'So we're back to someone who came here intending to murder Arthur,' said Freddie. 'But killing him in plain sight, in such an impossible manner, would take a lot of advance planning, wouldn't it?'

'Good point,' I said. 'But try this one on for size . . . Each one of you had a vested interest in the haunting of Harrow House turning out to be real. What if Arthur could have proved that it wasn't?'

'I didn't have any proof that it wasn't,' said Arthur.

'You all had something to lose,' I said, ignoring Arthur. 'If you spent the night in the most haunted house in Bath, and then had to admit in the morning that nothing happened, what would that do to your reputations? What better way to add to the mystery of Harrow House than to set up an impossible murder?'

'That makes no sense at all,' said Tom.

'Damn right!' said Freddie. 'We've experienced all kinds of strange stuff, and been made to see things that weren't actually there, by a force none of us understands. We didn't need to add anything; Harrow House is weird enough as it is.'

'Ah, well,' I said, 'it was just a theory. No doubt we'll work our way through a whole lot more before morning.'

'But you do accept that supernatural events have occurred in this house tonight?' said Freddie.

I was careful not to look at Arthur.

'Something is definitely going on here,' I said. 'But there's no hard evidence yet as to what it might be.'

Freddie snorted loudly. 'You're as bad as Tom. You want to fit everything into neat little boxes and nail down the lids. Science doesn't have all the answers. Neither does magic, but at least we're honest about it.'

'I don't need *all* the answers,' I said. 'Just a few would do.'

'If we can't come up with a motive,' said Tom, 'maybe we'll have better luck with opportunity. We were all right there with Arthur when he died, and some of us were closer than others.'

'Why are you looking at me?' said Lynn. 'Arthur was holding my hand when he died, and Ishmael had hold of my other hand. There was no way I could have done anything!'

'None of us could,' said Freddie.

'But no one else could have got to him,' said Tom. He frowned, thinking hard. 'We were all concentrating on the darkness in the doorway . . . Could someone have set that up to make sure we wouldn't see exactly how Arthur died?'

I raised a mental eyebrow at that. Why would Tom ask the question when he was the only one with the scientific background to arrange such a thing?

'It's clear from your recording that the dark was just the house messing with our heads,' said Freddie. 'Or are you suggesting the house is connected to the killer in some way?'

'Give me time,' said Tom. 'It's just a theory . . .'

'The dark only distracted us for a few moments,' said Lynn. 'How could anyone have killed Arthur that quickly? I still say he died of fright. He simply didn't have our experience when the moment came to face the unknown.'

'I was not scared!' Arthur said loudly. 'I was just interested! I know . . . *hush*.'

'So we can't prove opportunity,' Tom said heavily. 'That just leaves method. How could Arthur have been killed?'

He looked around hopefully, but no one had anything to offer. Lynn looked coldly at me.

'You're hiding something, Ishmael. I can tell.'

'You don't have to be psychic to guess that,' I said easily. 'But it's nothing to do with Arthur's death. Penny and I were sent here by a private security operation, in case someone was trying to use this house's reputation to embarrass our client, the prospective buyer.'

Lynn shook her head. She had that strange fey look in her eyes again.

'There's something out of the ordinary about you,' she said slowly, almost dreamily. 'As though there's more to you than the rest of us.'

'I said that!' said Freddie.

'But what does it mean?' said Tom.

Lynn fixed me with her unblinking gaze. Her eyes were very bright, in their dark bed of mascara. 'Ishmael isn't just Ishmael. There's someone else, looking out from behind his eyes . . .'

'OK . . .' said Freddie. 'Someone needs a time-out and a lie down with a cold cloth over their eyes.'

'I suggest we all take a break,' I said. 'And give some serious thought to what we've been discussing.'

Everyone settled back down in their chairs, intent on their own thoughts. No one looked obviously guilty, or even particularly innocent. I looked hopefully at Penny, sitting stiffly in the chair furthest from me, but she was still refusing to make eye contact. I turned to Arthur.

'Don't look at me,' he said immediately. 'I'm as baffled by what's going on as the rest of you.'

'You've been watching their auras,' I said. 'Was anyone lying?'

'Not as such,' said Arthur. 'It was more like they were all choosing their words really carefully, so they wouldn't have to lie. If you want my opinion, every single one of them looks guilty as hell. Though that could just be me. Ever since I was murdered, I've not been in the most generous of moods.'

'Were you ever?' I said.

'Leave me alone. I'm dead. I'm allowed to be grumpy.'

'Don't you want to help find your killer?'

'You know I do!' Arthur kicked a chair in his frustration, and then swore viciously as his foot sailed right through it. 'But this kind of thing isn't what I do! I'm a journalist, not a detective. Or at least I was. I was a lot of things that I'll never be again. I used to be all about doing the research and talking to the right people, and then putting the pieces together until I had a story, but we don't have the time or the resources for that. I'm not much use to you as a partner, am I?' He sighed heavily, which was actually quite disturbing from someone who didn't need to breathe. 'Look . . . Ishmael . . . go and make up with Penny. You need her.'

I looked at Penny. It seemed like a very long way to the other side of the room.

'She feels bad about being apart from you,' Arthur said

quietly. 'I don't need to read her aura to know that. I lost my chance with Freddie; don't you make the same mistake.'

I nodded, and walked steadily over to stand before Penny. She looked right through me.

'Penny?' I said. 'We need to talk.'

She still wouldn't acknowledge me, so I sat down heavily on the arm of her chair. The whole thing tilted sideways under my weight, and Penny had to throw her weight in the opposite direction to keep the chair from toppling over. She still refused to look at me.

'Not for the first time,' I said quietly, 'you were right, and I was wrong. I have run away from people I cared for, because I thought it was more important to protect the secret of what I am. And I have outlived many of the people I've known, because I don't come with the same sell-by date as everyone else. But you're different, Penny. You are the only person I have ever opened up to completely. The only one who knows everything about me – or as much as I know, at least. I will never walk away from you, because you help keep me human. By loving me, as I love you. And I won't give that up for anything.'

Penny finally turned around in her chair and looked at me. Her face wasn't giving anything away.

'Go on,' she said.

'I don't age like you do,' I said. 'At some point you will grow old and die, and I will go on. Whether I want to or not. But given the kind of lives we lead, and the kind of cases we work, it seems far more likely that we'll die together, trying to take down something far more dangerous than we are.'

Penny smiled slightly. 'Where are you going with this, Ishmael?'

'I have no idea what the future holds,' I said. 'So let's embrace our time together, because it could all be taken away from us at any moment. Just like Arthur.'

Penny got up out of her chair, and I stood up to face her. She reached out to me, and I took her in my arms. We held each other tightly, as though to make it clear to the universe that nothing was ever going to separate us.

There was the sound of polite applause from the rest of the room. When Penny and I finally let go of each other and looked around, Lynn and Freddie and Tom were looking quietly pleased that we weren't arguing any more. If only because it was one less distraction. Arthur grinned broadly and gave us a big thumbs up.

'We are back!' said Penny, smiling widely at me. 'The old partnership rides again! Just as well, really; it was actually painful watching you stumbling around and getting nowhere, trying to run an interrogation without me.'

I had to raise an eyebrow. 'You know, I did have a perfectly successful career before I met you.'

'It's a wonder to me you survived this long,' Penny said briskly. And then she looked at me thoughtfully. 'What was all that muttering and glancing off to one side?'

'I needed a partner,' I said. 'So I asked Arthur to help.'

Penny's eyes widened, and she put a hand to her mouth. It couldn't quite conceal her broad grin.

'You've been talking with a ghost, about his own murder?'

'Yes. He wasn't very helpful.'

'I heard that!' Arthur said loudly.

Penny's mouth pursed thoughtfully. 'Given that Arthur is a ghost, could he tell us anything about the true nature of Harrow House?'

'I suppose so,' I said. 'I never got around to asking him.'

'You see!' said Penny. 'This is why you need me. Where is he?'

I led her over to the fireplace, where Arthur was standing under the portrait of bad old Malcolm Welles. He nodded cheerfully to both of us. The others watched Penny and me carefully to see what we were up to, but when all we did was look solemnly at the portrait, they went back to their brooding. I indicated to Penny where Arthur was standing, and she nodded briskly in his general direction.

'Have you seen any other ghosts in this house, Arthur?'

'I did think to ask him that,' I said. 'Apparently, he's too scared to look.'

'I am not scared!' Arthur said immediately. 'It's just that the very idea disturbs the crap out of me.'

'What's he saying?' said Penny, taking in the look on my face. 'Ishmael, if this is going to work, you have to tell me everything he says.'

I brought her up to speed, and she looked sharply in Arthur's direction.

'But you're a ghost! What have you got to be worried about? You'd just be meeting someone who's in the same position as yourself. You'd probably find you have a lot in common.'

Arthur shuffled his feet awkwardly. They didn't make a sound.

'It's not that simple. Ever since I came back, I've been getting this . . . feeling that there are other things which exist on the same spiritual plane as me. Spiritual monsters that prey on the newly dead. Things so far beyond human understanding that we don't even have concepts for what they are.'

I leaned forward, intrigued. 'And you think there are things like that here, in Harrow House?'

'I don't know, and I don't want to find out. So I am not going to stick my head above the parapet, or make a lot of noise, or anything else that might get them looking in my direction.'

Penny listened impatiently as I explained the long pause, and then sniffed loudly.

'How much of this do you actually know, Arthur, and how much is just you having a fit of the vapours?'

'Which one of us is dead, and therefore the authority on this whole afterlife situation?' Arthur said huffily. 'Most of my senses are gone now; all I have are my feelings.'

'But given that you are very definitely dead, if not actually departed, what else could happen to you?' I said reasonably.

'I don't know!' said Arthur. 'That's what scares me.'

Penny did her best to appear sympathetic but couldn't hide her impatience.

'It sounds more to me like you're having a panic attack, Arthur. Do you need to breathe into a paper bag or something?'

'He doesn't breathe,' I said.

'All right,' said Penny. 'Arthur! Try sticking your head between your knees. Or under your arm.'

Arthur looked at me. 'One more remark like that, and I will hit her with a rain of frogs. Right here, right now.'

'Ishmael? Why are you smiling like that?' said Penny.

'Let me talk to him,' I said. 'Arthur, just try to reach out and get a sense of what's actually going on in Harrow House. You don't have to give away where you are; just spy on things, from a distance.'

'I can do that,' said Arthur. 'I'm a journalist. In spirit, anyway.'

'In particular, we need to know if some form of intelligence might be trapped in this house,' I said.

Arthur looked at me sharply. 'What connection could that possibly have to how I was murdered?'

'Until we find out what's really going on, how can we be sure of anything?' I said reasonably. 'Give it your best shot.'

He looked at me for a long moment. 'I am curious as to exactly what it was that drove my ancestors out, all those years ago. And screwed up my family for generations afterwards. OK! What's the use of being dead if you can't discover the truth about the things that matter, and maybe arrange for a little karmic payback?'

'Now you're talking,' I said.

'Hush,' he said, grinning.

He concentrated, frowning so hard it would have hurt his face if he had still been alive. He stared at the closed door, and then through it, as though his mind was roaming the rest of the house. Something in his face reminded me of the fey quality I'd glimpsed in Lynn earlier, and while I was still trying to work out what that might mean, Arthur suddenly relaxed and shook his head firmly.

'I'm not picking up anything. Not even the bad vibrations that affected us all when we entered the house. If there is some old-time presence still hanging around here, it must have disappeared into a hole and then dragged the hole in after it, because I'm getting nothing.'

'Why would it want to hide from us?' I said.

'Why would what want to hide from us?' said Penny. 'Ishmael, what is Arthur saying?'

I filled her in on the details. Penny frowned.

'Perhaps whatever it is decided that since the usual scare

tactics aren't working, the best thing for it to do is keep its head down until we've all left.'

'You think it's scared of us?' I said.

Penny shrugged. 'Maybe it never had to cope with a murder and a new ghost on the same night before.'

'You think it might be scared of *me*?' said Arthur, beaming widely. 'Damn. I am proud . . .'

A thought struck me. 'Arthur, did you see the stuffed animals we thought were talking to us earlier?'

'No,' he said immediately. 'I wondered what was going on there.' He stopped to think about that for a moment. 'If I couldn't see or hear them, that's presumably because I'm dead and therefore don't have a living mind to be fooled . . . But on the other hand, I don't think I like the idea of things going on around me that I don't know about.'

'If you can't see them, then that has to mean there isn't anything going on,' I said patiently.

'Oh. Yes. I think . . .'

'Whatever is at the heart of Harrow House's bad reputation,' I said, 'must derive from the original bad thing that happened to Malcolm Welles and his family.'

'It's sounding more and more to me as though Malcolm was the real villain of the piece,' said Penny. 'Could he have compelled something unnatural to serve him, and then imprisoned it here, until finally it got the chance to break free?'

'Hold it right there,' said Arthur. 'Did you just say *unnatural*? Are we talking about Malcolm making a deal with the Devil, in return for success in business? OK, that is it: I am disappearing and not coming back until all of this is over.'

'We don't know anything of the sort,' I said reassuringly. 'Malcolm might have made a deal with something else entirely.'

'Like what?' said Arthur.

'Something not of this world,' I said.

'Oh, come on!' said Arthur. 'Really?'

I gave him my best hard look. 'You have no problem with your ancestor making a deal with the Devil, but you draw the line at aliens?'

'Yes! No! I don't know!' Arthur scowled unhappily. 'This

all sounds like silly-season stuff to me . . . You honestly think my ancestor had a really close encounter, stole some alien's knowledge to give him an unfair advantage in business, and then locked it up here in this house so no one would ever find out? And it's still here? That is a hell of a lot of ifs and maybes . . .'

'But it would explain why Malcolm and his family had to run like hell when the alien finally broke loose,' I said. 'I'm guessing it wouldn't have been in the best of moods by then.'

'But if the alien did break free, why didn't it leave the house and go after him?' said Penny after she'd caught up.

'Malcolm must have had some other way to hold it here,' I said. 'Which is why it's never been able to leave the house.'

'And you think it's still alive, after all these years?' said Penny.

'Who knows how long an alien could live?' I said.

Penny and I exchanged a look and a smile.

'What was that?' Arthur said quickly. 'I saw that! What just happened there?'

'Private joke,' I said briskly. 'Now, Arthur, is there anything about the original story you can tell us, something that only your family might have known? Any detail, no matter how small, that they never shared with anyone outside the family?'

Arthur thought about it. 'On the rare occasions when my family did talk about the house, I always made a point of not listening. As a form of rebellion – to make it clear I didn't want Harrow House dominating my life. But now I wonder whether my family never talked about it when I was around, because they knew I didn't want to know.

'When I got older, I did start to take an interest. I wanted to know what it was that had blighted my family's life for so long. But when I finally started asking questions, I was surprised to discover my family really didn't know much after all. Previous generations had done all they could to bury the story, trying to put it behind them.

'When I started working for the *Bath Herald*, I made use of their archives, so I could read the original stories, but they turned out to be mainly gossip and hearsay – most of it concerning the treasure Malcolm was supposed to have abandoned in his hurry to get away. I'm starting to think now that maybe he did leave something behind, but it was a prisoner, rather than treasure . . .

'The only detail I can think of is that something was supposed to have happened down in the cellar, right before Malcolm and his family ran for their lives. It's not actually a secret, just a detail that was only mentioned in one of the original accounts.'

'Then that's where we have to go,' I said. 'Down into the cellar, to see if something is still there.'

'What's this *we* stuff?' Arthur said loudly. 'I'm not going down there! Why would I want to go down there?'

'Don't you want to learn the truth at last?' I said.

'Well, yes, but on the other hand, a whole lot of not necessarily,' said Arthur.

'The three of us together are perfectly capable of taking on anything that might still be lurking in a cellar,' I said.

'Can I have that in writing?' said Arthur.

'Ishmael and I have experience when it comes to dealing with the weird and uncanny,' said Penny, after I'd explained Arthur's reluctance. 'We kick monster arse for a living.'

Arthur sighed. 'You know, there was a time I would have moved heaven and hell to get to the bottom of a comment like that, but now it's just another story I'll never get to write.'

'There's nothing to worry about,' I said. 'You're the ghost this house is scared of, remember?'

'I'm finding that idea less and less convincing,' said Arthur. 'Oh, hell . . . Let us do this brave and incredibly stupid thing, before we all have a rush of common sense to the head and do something sane instead.'

'That's the spirit,' I said briskly. 'Now, how do we get down to the cellar?'

'I don't know,' said Arthur.

I looked at him. 'What do you mean, you don't know?'

He glared right back at me. 'How many times do I have to say this? I have never been inside this house before! I don't know where anything is. And I definitely didn't see a door anywhere in the hallway that might lead down to a cellar.'

'Is he saying he doesn't know where the cellar is?' said Penny. 'How can he not know? Arthur . . .'

'I'm over here,' Arthur said coldly.

I turned Penny so she was pointing in the right direction, and she put on her most winning smile.

'Arthur, when you first felt the unpleasant atmosphere in this house, where did it start?'

'Right by the front door,' said Arthur. 'You know that; you were there!'

I explained to Penny, and she nodded quickly.

'So, clearly, that is where we need to start looking,' said Penny. 'Ishmael, should we tell the others what we're doing?'

'Best not to,' I said. 'We don't want to put them at risk.'

'Risk?' Arthur said quickly. 'What risk?'

'We're going to have to tell them something,' said Penny.

We looked round at the others, just in time to see Tom heading for the door.

'Tom?' I said. 'Where are you off to?'

He stopped and brandished an empty water bottle. 'I need to take a leak. Thought I'd do it in one of the other rooms.'

Arthur bristled. 'I am not having him take a piss in front of my body!'

'What difference would it make?' I said.

'It's not nice,' said Arthur.

I turned my attention back to Tom. 'I don't think you should go anywhere on your own. Not in this house.'

'Damn right,' said Freddie. 'What did I say earlier about the fate of supporting actors in horror movies?'

'I'll be fine,' said Tom. 'And I don't want anyone coming with me, thank you. This is not the kind of performance that benefits from an audience. I'll leave this door ajar, and the door to the room I choose, so I can call for help if I need it.' He paused. 'You would come if I called, wouldn't you?'

'Of course,' said Freddie. 'If only out of curiosity.'

'Do you have another empty bottle?' said Lynn.

'Could you manage with a bottle?' said Tom.

She scowled at him. 'I'll have to, won't I? Just hand it over, and I'll use whichever room you don't.'

'Now *she* wants to piss in front of me!' said Arthur.

'It's really not a good idea for both of us to be going off on our own,' said Tom. 'You stay put, and I'll sort you out another bottle when I get back.'

He quickly left the room, leaving the door ajar. I hurried over and eased the door open a little more, so I could peer cautiously past it. Penny and Arthur moved in behind me.

'What are you two doing?' said Freddie.

'Just checking to make sure he's all right,' I said.

'He was definitely being evasive,' said Arthur. 'You should have seen his aura; it was all over the place.'

'I was able to work that one out on my own,' I said. 'I wonder what he's really up to . . .'

'Must be something pretty important, to send him off on his own in a house like this,' said Penny.

'But what could be so important that he didn't want to talk about it?' I said.

'Maybe he's meeting someone,' said Arthur.

I watched Tom enter the right-hand room and close the door firmly behind him. I stepped out into the empty hall, and Penny was quickly there at my side. Lynn and Freddie immediately rose up out of their chairs.

'What's going on?' said Freddie.

'You're not going off and leaving us, are you?' said Lynn.

'We're just going down the hall a way, to keep an eye on Tom,' I said. 'You stay put, and we'll be back before you know it.'

I gestured for Arthur to come and join Penny and me, but he hesitated before the open doorway.

'I can't leave this room, remember? The house won't let me.'

'Stick close to us and you should be fine,' I said. 'I have a strong feeling this house wants its secret discovered at last.'

'So now you're having feelings?' said Arthur.

He braced himself and stepped through the doorway. Nothing stopped him. I gave him a reassuring smile and pulled the door shut behind us.

SIX
What's in the Cellar?

The hall was as brightly lit as it should be, open and empty and very quiet. It was trying hard to look innocent, but I wasn't buying it. Penny and Arthur stood on either side of me, as we looked down the long hallway to the front door. I turned to Arthur.

'Are you seeing anything that Penny and I might be missing? Are you feeling anything out of the ordinary?'

Arthur shuffled his feet uncomfortably, and it still bothered me that they didn't make a sound.

'There's nothing ordinary about Harrow House,' he said slowly. 'I'm not seeing anything that you're not . . . but I am getting a feeling that something is waiting for us, down by the front door. Something we missed when we first arrived.'

Penny squeezed my arm hard until I looked at her. 'Arthur's saying something, isn't he? You have to keep me in the loop, Ishmael! How else can I stay on top of what's happening? Or what seems to be happening . . . You know I hate being left out of things!'

'Trust me,' I said. 'You really don't want to hear everything he says.'

'Well, there's gratitude,' said Arthur.

I concentrated on Penny. 'Arthur thinks there's something important down by the front door.'

'I already worked that out from the expression on your face when you looked at the door,' said Penny. 'And that was my idea, anyway!'

'You see?' I said. 'You don't need me to tell you everything. Just watch me closely and be guided by me in all things.'

'Yeah, that's going to happen,' she said. 'I need you to talk to me, Ishmael; it's the principle of the thing!'

'Oh, if it's got down to principles, you're in trouble,' said

Arthur. 'A word to the wise, Ishmael: when you're in a hole, stop digging. Even if you do eventually win the argument, she'll still find a way to make you feel like you lost.'

I had to smile. 'You do know about women, after all.'

Arthur grinned. 'More than you do.'

'This whole conversation is at my expense, isn't it?' said Penny.

'Let's go take a look at the front door,' I said.

'I still think we would have spotted another door when we first came in,' said Arthur.

'In this house?' I said. 'There could have been a doorway big enough to accommodate an elephant with a hunchback, along with a big flashing neon sign pointing straight to it, saying *Secret Door Right Here!* and this house could still have kept us from noticing.'

Penny patted my arm comfortingly. 'Keep the noise level down, darling. The point is: why would it want to?'

'I think the more pertinent question is: why are we being allowed to look for it now?' I said. 'It's always possible that we are being lured into a trap.'

'Wouldn't be the first time,' said Penny. 'And anyway, I like traps. You know where you are, then. And it's always such fun breaking out of them.'

'She's very confident, isn't she?' said Arthur.

I gestured at the open hallway. 'Since you see and feel so much, and because you are already mortally challenged, Arthur, you can lead the way.'

He scowled. 'Why did I just know you were going to say that?'

'Maybe you're psychic, as well as a ghost,' I said.

'I loathe you more than words can say,' said Arthur.

He set off down the hall, his feet making no sound at all on the bare wooden floorboards. Penny and I strolled after him, keeping a cautious watch on our surroundings. Halfway down the hall I stopped suddenly, and Penny stopped with me. Arthur carried on for a few moments before realizing he was on his own, and then he came hurrying back to join us.

'What?' he said loudly. 'What's happened and why didn't I notice it? Should I be worried? I mean, more than usual.'

I gestured at the door to the right-hand room. 'I saw Tom go in there . . . but I'm not hearing anything from inside that room.'

'Well, that's hardly surprising, is it?' said Arthur. 'The door's shut. Even though he said he'd leave it open. He must be shyer than he thought.'

'I should still be able to hear him,' I said. 'Even with the door closed.'

'Seriously?' said Arthur.

'Yes,' I said.

'Ishmael could hear a fish fart in a fountain,' Penny said proudly.

'How often does that come in handy?' said Arthur.

I moved right up to the door, pressed my face against the jamb and sniffed deeply.

'OK . . .' said Arthur. 'You are seriously creeping me out now. Why do you need to smell him? And how could you anyway, through a crack in the door?'

'I'm very well trained,' I said, not looking around. 'Or part bloodhound. Choose whichever explanation makes you feel easier.'

His eyes narrowed. 'My keen journalistic instincts are telling me there is something seriously out of the ordinary about you, Ishmael . . . That you are almost certainly not going to explain to me.'

'Got it in one,' I said. I pressed my ear against the door. 'I can't hear him moving about. Can't hear him breathing, or the rustling of his clothes.'

Arthur stared determinedly off into the distance. 'Not going to ask . . .'

'And I'm not smelling even a hint of piss.'

'Not listening, la la la . . .'

'Could something have happened to Tom?' said Penny. 'Perhaps he's collapsed, as well.'

'You think he might be a ghost now?' said Arthur. 'I'm not sure how I feel about that. It would be nice to have someone else to talk to, but did it have to be him?'

'We'd better check this out,' I said. 'I'll only worry otherwise.'

'What if he still has . . . matters in hand?' said Arthur.

'He hasn't,' I said. 'I'd know.'

'You're weird,' said Arthur.

I opened the door and strode into the room, with Penny at my side and Arthur reluctantly bringing up the rear, if only because he didn't want to be left alone out in the hall. The room was completely empty, apart from the various bits of furniture lurking under dust sheets. There was no sign of Tom anywhere. I could only be sure he'd come into the room because the light was still on, and because his empty water bottle was standing on a dusty side table.

'Where is he?' said Penny, peering quickly about her. 'There's no other door, no window . . . nowhere he could have gone. Did the house disappear him?'

'Hardly,' Arthur said smugly. 'Look at the floor.'

A single set of footprints showed clearly in the thick layer of dust, leading all the way to the furthest wall and then stopping abruptly. As though Tom had walked right through it. I pointed the trail out to Penny, and she nodded slowly.

'Now, that really is spooky. Have we got another ghost on our hands?'

'I think we're looking at sneaky, rather than spooky,' said Arthur. 'There's a sliding panel in that wall, giving access to a secret hiding place. I told you: treasure-seekers have been all over this house for decades. So many they were practically tripping over each other for a while. This particular secret panel hasn't been a secret for ages.' And then he stopped and scowled thoughtfully at the wall. 'Except . . . It's been so long since any treasure-seekers came poking around here that maybe the secret's so old it's new again.'

I followed the footsteps to where they stopped right before the wall, and then leaned forward to study the wood panelling. Delicately carved scrollwork decorated each panel, all but invisible under the thick layers of dust. Penny moved in beside me and lowered her voice.

'Do you think Tom is hiding somewhere inside the wall?'

'I know he is,' I said. 'I can hear him breathing.' I looked back at Arthur. 'What is there, behind this panel?'

'Just a small concealed space,' he said. 'No telling what it was originally intended for – most likely things Malcolm didn't want the tax people to know about. And I think rich people just liked having secret sliding panels in their walls back in those days. Something they could show off to visitors. If there ever was anything valuable stored in that space, you can bet someone spirited it away long ago . . . Though I'm guessing Tom didn't know that.'

He stepped forward and thrust his immaterial head through the wall, right up to the shoulders. I thought about calling him back, and then had to wonder if he'd hear me. He pulled his head out and grinned at me.

'Yeah, he's in there. Standing really still and holding his breath, hoping we'll give up and go away.'

'How do you open the panel?' I said.

Arthur pointed to a descending row of roses on the wood-work. 'Third from the top. Hit it hard; the mechanism's bound to be a bit stiff.'

I pressed the rose firmly, and a door-sized panel slid sideways, disappearing into the wall. A shocked and startled Tom stared out at us from a room not much bigger than a cupboard.

'Hello, Tom,' I said. 'Did you really need to go to such lengths, just so you could take a leak in private?'

'Ah . . .' said Tom.

'Get out of there,' I said. 'Don't make me come in after you.'

Tom quickly emerged, smiling weakly at me and Penny.

'How did you know where to find me?'

'Arthur told me about the sliding panel,' I said. 'The question is: what were you doing in there?'

'Well, I was . . .'

'No,' I said. 'Try again.'

His shoulders slumped. 'All right! I was looking for Malcolm Welles's lost treasure. That's the real reason I came here. I arranged to get myself picked as part of this group, over much better-qualified people, by bribing one of the estate agents to say I had special knowledge of the house and its history.'

'And I thought you were all about the science,' I said. 'Dedicated to the search for hard evidence of the afterlife.'

'I am!' Tom said immediately. 'Most of the time. But do you

have any idea how expensive that kind of specialized equipment is? I ran through all my savings long ago, with nothing to show for it. And you have to keep upgrading your tech, or the field will leave you behind. When I heard about tonight's investigation, I just knew Harrow House was my best hope, and my last chance. Either to find a ghost or discover treasure that could keep me going for years.

'When the weird stuff started happening, I thought, *Finally! This is it!* And I had it all recorded, as proof. I could write a book, go on a speaking tour, maybe even get some corporate funding at last. My own television show! But then you had to go and prove that most of what we experienced wouldn't record, and I had nothing . . . So all I had left was my original plan.'

'What made you so sure there was still some treasure here?' I said. 'And how did you know about the sliding panel?'

Tom smiled. 'I read about the hidden wall space in a book I picked up at a ghost-hunters convention. Malcolm Welles's original diary. The seller didn't know what he had, but I did.'

Arthur laughed derisively. 'There have been any number of fake Malcolm Welles diaries down the years! For a while there, turning out copies of the diary was a thriving cottage industry. Anyone who'd done their proper research on Harrow House would have known that.'

'The old-time treasure-hunters cleaned out this wall space long ago,' I said to Tom. 'According to Arthur.'

Tom shook his head slowly. 'Typical of my luck . . . So, what are you going to do? I haven't broken any laws. But if you tell anyone about this, my reputation in the ghost-chasing fraternity will be ruined.'

Penny looked at me. 'This isn't what we came here for, Ishmael.'

'You're right,' I said. 'It's just another distraction.' I looked sternly at Tom. 'Go back to the far room. Give your empty water bottle to the ladies, and tell them to use it where they are. While you stand guard outside the door, like the good gentleman you are. When they're done, you can go in and wait with them until we come back.'

'What will you be doing, while we're waiting?' said Tom.

I gave him a hard look and he actually backed away, holding up his hands defensively. 'Right! Of course! None of my business.'

'Do as you're told and stay out of our way, and we'll pretend none of this ever happened,' I said.

Tom nodded quickly, grabbed his water bottle and hurried out of the room before I could change my mind. I studied the open space in the wall. The cupboard appeared to be entirely bare. I turned to Arthur.

'Can you see anything of interest in there?'

'Not a thing,' said Arthur. And then he turned slowly, almost reluctantly, to stare at the door leading out into the hall. 'But I can hear something. Like a voice, calling to me . . . and I think it's getting impatient.'

'Then let's go find out what it is,' I said.

I led the way out of the room, and all the way down the hall to the front door. Penny strode along beside me, while Arthur slouched along in the rear. When we finally reached the door, the first thing I did was check to see if it was still locked. It was.

'We're not going anywhere,' said Penny. 'This house isn't finished with us yet.'

'I wish you'd stop saying things like that!' said Arthur. 'You're not doing my nerves any good. Ishmael, tell her to stop saying things like that.'

'It's bad enough having to pass on your information,' I said. 'I'm not including your personal comments. Now concentrate, Arthur; what do you feel?'

Almost against his will, his head turned slowly to look at the left-hand wall next to the front door. He drifted over to stand before it.

'There!' he said, pointing suddenly.

And just like that, I was looking at a door in the wall that definitely hadn't been there a moment before. A perfectly ordinary, real and very solid-looking door.

'Where did that come from?' said Penny.

'It was here all along,' I said. 'We just weren't being allowed to see it, until now.'

Penny frowned. 'So what's changed since we were last here?'

I turned to Arthur. 'It has to be you. When we first entered the house, you were still alive. Perhaps now that you're dead, the house can make contact through you.'

'You are seriously freaking me out,' said Arthur. 'Are you saying the house killed me, just so it could have someone to talk to?'

'No,' I said. 'One of our little group did that.'

'How can you be so sure?' said Arthur.

'Because I pay attention,' I said.

Arthur let that one go. 'Why is the house so reliant on me?'

'Something to do with your family connections?' I said. 'Or perhaps because I can see you . . .'

'What's so special about you?' said Arthur.

'I don't think Harrow House has ever encountered anyone like me,' I said. 'Perhaps it's curious. Either way, it would seem that whatever's down in the cellar wants you to bring me to it.'

'You really believe something's still alive down there, after all these years?' said Penny.

'Alien life spans,' I said. 'Remember?'

'There's an *alien* in the cellar?' said Arthur, his voice rising.

'Wouldn't surprise me,' I said.

I tried the handle, but the door wouldn't open. I rattled it so hard the door shook in its frame, but it still wouldn't cooperate. The lock was a large and very solid steel affair.

'Of course it's locked,' I said. 'It would be too easy, otherwise.'

'I thought we were invited?' said Penny.

'Maybe it can't unlock the door,' I said. 'That's why it's still trapped down there – why it needs us . . . So it can finally get out and leave Harrow House.'

'Letting out some unknown and probably very angry alien creature doesn't sound like such a great idea to me,' Penny said carefully. 'Whatever's down there sent Malcolm and his family screaming in horror from this house, Ishmael, back in 1889. It's been brooding and planning ever since. And if it did kill Arthur, just so it could communicate through him . . .'

'My word, is that the time?' said Arthur. 'I really must be going . . .'

'Stand where you are,' I said sternly.

'What would you do if I didn't?'

'I could leave you alone,' I said. 'And then who would you have to talk to?'

'Bully,' muttered Arthur.

'Sorry,' I said. 'Blame it on the house. Now stop being a wimp, and stick your head through that door. We need to know what's on the other side.'

Arthur looked at his feet, rather than at the door. 'That really doesn't feel like something I should do.'

'Why not?' I said. 'It worked with the sliding panel.'

'That was different,' said Arthur. 'There's no telling what there might be on the other side of this door. What if I get stuck? What if something grabs hold of my head and won't let go?'

'How would they do that?' I said reasonably.

'I don't know! That's what's so worrying!'

'Were you like this when you were alive?' I said. 'I thought you were a big brave investigative reporter?'

He scowled. 'All I had to worry about then was editors and deadlines.'

'Get on with it,' I said.

'Rest in peace, my arse,' said Arthur. 'I haven't had a moment's peace since I was forcefully shuffled off this mortal coil.'

He stuck his head through the door and then quickly jerked it back out again.

'Nothing there!' he said, looking very relieved. 'Just darkness.'

'That isn't necessarily a good thing,' I said. 'Remember the dark in the door, just before you were killed?'

'The two aren't necessarily connected,' Penny said quickly, as she picked up the gist of the conversation.

'You can't be sure of that,' said Arthur, backing away from the door. 'I don't think I want any more to do with this.'

'I don't think you have a choice,' I said, as kindly as I could. 'The house let you out of the other room because it has a use for you. If you upset it, you could end up trapped in that room again. Or, possibly, somewhere worse.'

'Back off, Ishmael,' said Penny. 'Don't press him.' She smiled in Arthur's general direction. 'If the house has been using you, then this is your best chance to break its hold on you. Because whatever's down in the cellar, Ishmael and I will stand with you when you face it, and do whatever it takes to shut it down.'

Arthur nodded slowly. 'OK . . . How are we going to get past the door? That lock looks pretty substantial. Or do you have some kind of special security lock-picks?'

'Something like that,' I said.

I took careful aim, pivoted on one foot and unleashed a devastating kick with the other foot. My heel punched the solid steel lock right out of the door and dropped it on the other side. Penny jumped up and down, whooping loudly and applauding. Arthur's jaw dropped. I was left standing balanced on one foot, while my other foot remained wedged in the hole in the door where the lock had been. I tugged a few times, but my foot wouldn't budge. I looked to Penny.

'If you wouldn't mind . . .'

She grasped the situation immediately and moved in close so I could take hold of her shoulder. Properly anchored, I was able to jerk my foot out of the hole and stand properly again.

'Did that kick hurt, sweetie?' said Penny.

'Like you wouldn't believe,' I said.

'Try not to limp. It would only undermine your image.'

'I have an image?'

Arthur stopped studying the ragged hole I'd made in the thick wood of the door, and gave me his full attention.

'How the hell did you do that?'

'I eat my spinach.'

I pushed the door open. Light from the hallway illuminated the beginnings of a set of stone steps, falling down into darkness. My eyes pierced the gloom for some of the way, suggesting that at least this time we were dealing with a perfectly ordinary darkness. I was able to make out a single bare light bulb hanging above the steps, so I fumbled around inside the doorway until I found the switch and turned it on. Dull yellow light splashed along the rough stone walls lining the stairway.

Arthur stepped forward, just a bit gingerly, and looked down the steps.

'Something is definitely down there,' he said quietly. 'It feels . . . strange.' He shook his head, frowning. 'I can't seem to get a grip on it – as though it's too big to get my head around. I really don't like the way it's making me feel . . .'

'I don't like the way it's been making all of us feel,' I said. 'In fact, I intend to have some very strong words with whatever's down there, just to make my displeasure extremely clear.'

I strode through Arthur and started down the steps. Penny followed right behind me, also walking through Arthur, though she didn't know it.

'I hate it when you do that!' Arthur said loudly. 'Just because I'm dead, it doesn't mean I don't have feelings! Respect my spiritual space!'

'Try to keep up,' I said, not looking back.

'I'm right here,' said Penny.

'I was talking to Arthur,' I said.

'Oh,' she said. 'What's he saying now?'

I listened for a moment. 'You really don't want to know.'

We were halfway down before Arthur caught up with us. I couldn't hear his feet on the steps, but his grumpy voice was suddenly that much closer.

'What do you suppose it is that's waiting for us? Some kind of creature from outer space – all thrashing tentacles, big blobby eyes, and lots of mouths packed full of teeth . . .'

'I saw that movie,' I said. 'I wasn't convinced.'

'Doesn't mean I'm wrong,' said Arthur. 'This thing has been scaring the crap out of the local people for generations.'

'If it's been trapped in the cellar since 1889, it's hardly going to be in the best of moods,' I said.

Arthur sniffed loudly. 'All the more reason not to barge in where it lives, and upset it.'

I realized Penny was glaring at me, feeling left out again. I shot her a reassuring smile, but it didn't seem to help much.

'Arthur is worried,' I said.

'Imagine my surprise,' said Penny.

'Everything's going to be fine, Arthur,' I said. 'Penny and

I have lots of experience when it comes to dealing with extra-terrestrials.'

'You have experience?' said Arthur. 'What kind of experience?'

'Don't ask,' I said.

He sniffed again. 'Like it would do any good.'

Penny shook her head. 'It's like listening to someone talking on their phone on the train.'

'And I know how much you love that,' I said.

'Am I missing anything important?' Penny said pointedly.

'Not really,' I said.

Penny stared down the steps. 'How much further does this go? We must be deep under the house by now.'

'I think a more interesting question might be: why did Malcolm need a cellar this far underground?' I said.

'Because he was scared of what he had incarcerated down here?' said Penny.

'Seems likely,' I said.

'And we're heading straight for it,' said Arthur. 'I always knew there was a good reason why I never wanted anything to do with this house.'

We'd almost reached the bottom of the steps when the atmosphere of dread and horror suddenly hit us again. It fell on us like a great weight, and I had to stop where I was so I could force the awful feelings back to a bearable level. Penny gripped my arm with both hands, her eyes squeezed tightly shut. Arthur moaned sickly.

'Why is it doing this?' he said. 'We're doing what it wants, aren't we? And how am I even able to feel this, now I'm dead?'

'I don't know,' I said. It took a lot of effort to speak calmly. 'Maybe there's more than one force operating in this house.'

'More than one alien?' said Arthur.

'More than one alien?' said Penny. She'd forced her eyes open, but I could see the terrible strain in her face.

'Maybe one alien . . . and something else,' I said.

'You're just full of these helpful little notions, aren't you?' said Arthur.

'We can't stay here, Ishmael,' said Penny. She had to struggle just to get a few words out. 'We have to go on.'

'Of course we do,' I said.

It took most of my strength and resolve to get moving again. Penny came with me, still clinging on to my arm with both hands. The steps ended at another door, just as ordinary as the one up above, except this door was standing half open. The darkness beyond it swallowed up the light from the steps and stopped it dead in its tracks. As though it wasn't welcome.

'Why is this door open?' said Arthur.

'Because we're expected?' I said.

'It could have been left that way, ever since the alien broke out,' said Penny.

'But why is it still open?' said Arthur.

'Perhaps because after it drove Malcolm and his family out, the alien discovered it couldn't leave the house and had to come back,' I said. 'Because this is all it knew. The nearest thing it had to a home, in this world.'

'Oh, that's just sad,' said Penny.

'Can I ask something?' said Arthur.

'At this point, I think I'd be shocked if you didn't,' I said. 'What's on your recently deceased mind, Arthur?'

'What if we're wrong?' he said bluntly. 'What if it isn't an alien? What if my ancestor really did make a deal with the Devil all those years ago . . . and what he summoned up is still here?'

'I don't believe in things like that,' I said.

'You didn't believe in ghosts until you met me.'

'The only way to find out is to go in there and face it,' I said. 'And then do whatever's necessary to bring the hammer down on it.'

'I wish I had your confidence,' Arthur said wistfully. 'It must be wonderful to be brave . . .'

'Are you still thinking about punching the alien in the face?' Penny said to me quietly. 'I mean, yes, you did very well with the door at the top of the stairs, but doors aren't renowned for their ability to fight back.'

'After everything the thing in the cellar has put us through, it needs cutting down to size,' I said. 'And if a good punch in the brains will stop it making me feel like this, I am quite definitely up for that.'

'All right,' said Penny, her voice entirely steady. 'You hit it from one side, and I'll come at it from the other.'

'Sounds like a plan to me,' I said.

'I'm dead, and I'm the sanest person here,' Arthur said sadly.

I gave the door a good hard shove, and it flew back to slam against the inner wall. Shadows jumped and then settled in a wide open room, only partially revealed by light spilling in from the stairway. I stepped cautiously into the cellar, and Penny and Arthur followed me in.

There was nobody home. Just four stone walls, a low ceiling and an uneven stone floor. No furniture, nothing left in storage – just the gloom and the shadows. But the atmosphere of dread and horror was just as strong, filling my head with terrible half-formed thoughts.

'After everything we've gone through to get here, we end up in an empty room?' said Penny. 'I was expecting a hideous monster, crouching in the remains of its cage, trailing its broken chains . . . But I can't see anything to suggest there was ever anything down here.'

'Something is here,' said Arthur. 'I can feel it. Watching and listening . . .'

'The atmosphere is getting worse,' said Penny, rubbing distractedly at her forehead. 'It feels as though I'm being driven out of my mind, by thoughts that don't make any sense. I don't know how much longer I can stand this . . .'

'Arthur!' I said sharply. 'Talk to me! What's happening in here?'

'It feels awful,' he said miserably. 'I didn't feel this bad when I was alive . . . It's like my head is full of insane voices shouting at each other.'

'This isn't us,' I said, glaring about me. 'These aren't our feelings or thoughts; they're being imposed on us from outside. Maybe . . . something left over, from when the alien was still here. A stone tape memory, being played back. The alien could be long dead, with only its memories remaining to haunt Harrow House. No . . . Wait. That's strange . . .'

'What is?' Arthur said immediately.

'What are you feeling, Ishmael?' said Penny. She was

leaning all her weight against me, as though I was the only thing holding her up.

'Something is trying to talk to me,' I said. 'But I can't understand anything it's saying.'

'Yes . . .' said Penny. 'My head is full of weird voices, drowning out my own thoughts.'

I turned my head slowly back and forth, and finally pointed at the far wall. 'It feels stronger in that direction.'

'And you're going to head straight for it, aren't you?' said Arthur.

'Of course,' I said. 'It's the only way to get to the truth.'

'How is it you're alive and I'm dead?' said Arthur.

I started towards the far wall and then stopped as I realized the others weren't coming with me. When I looked back, Penny was breathing hard and making low, pained noises, just from the effort involved in holding her ground. Arthur looked as if he might break and run at any moment.

'What's wrong?' I said.

'I can't go any closer,' said Penny. 'I just can't. It feels like walking towards my own death.'

'Worse than death,' said Arthur. 'It feels like horror and madness and the end of all things . . .'

'We've reached the heart of everything that's wrong with this house,' I said. 'I'm not turning back now. But I can't do it without you, Penny.'

I put out a hand to her, and she took hold and gripped it fiercely. Step by step she forced herself forward to join me, and then we just kept going until we were standing in front of the far wall. It was made up of different-sized stones, jammed in tight together without any need for mortar. A quick glance round confirmed the other walls had been put together in the same way. The work looked rushed, even amateurish.

The atmosphere was really bad now. Terrible thoughts sleeted through my mind, forced in from my surroundings. I'd found what I'd been looking for, and it was like finally looking God in the eye and discovering he's completely insane. I had to force myself to concentrate on the structure of the wall before me.

'I don't think this is the original cellar wall,' I said. 'It doesn't look strong enough. This was put in later.'

'Why would Malcolm do that?' said Penny. Her voice was firmer now, but she was squeezing my hand really hard. 'Was he trying to isolate what was in here?'

'Or maybe he wanted to hide something,' I said.

'Whatever's here is trying to drive us away,' said Penny. 'The voices are screaming inside my head . . .'

I snatched my gaze away from the stone wall, and when I looked at Penny, I saw all the colour had drained out of her face, and she was shaking hard.

'You don't have to be here,' I said. 'There's no reason why you should have to suffer this. I can handle what needs doing.'

'Like hell you can,' she said, glaring at me fiercely. 'You need me, to watch your back. I'll never leave you, Ishmael.'

'I'll never leave you,' I said.

'Given the chance, I'd leave both of you in a moment if I thought there was anywhere else to go,' said Arthur. 'But we are getting close to the truth. I can feel it.' He laughed briefly: a harsh, determined sound. 'I never ran away from a story in my life and I'm not about to start now I'm dead.'

He moved jerkily forward, step by step. Fighting his way through the horrible feelings flooding the room, almost snarling with the concentration it took, until finally he was standing beside us. He shot me a triumphant look and then glared at the cellar wall.

'There's something behind these stones. The source of everything that's wrong with Harrow House.'

I passed this on to Penny, and she looked at me sharply.

'Could it be walled-up bodies? Some kind of human sacrifice, in payment for Malcolm's success in business?'

'It's not bodies,' said Arthur. 'I'd know if it was bodies. Dead speaks to dead.'

I slowly eased my hand out of Penny's grasp, and she clasped her hands tightly together before her, shaking all over from the effort it took just to stay with me. I ran my hands over the rough, raised stones of the cellar wall, pulling and tugging at them until I found a loose one. I hauled it out and threw it to one side. I looked into the gap I'd made, and alien technology stared back at me.

Metal and crystal shapes, abstract almost beyond bearing, set in patterns that made no sense. Illuminated from within, they blazed in colours I didn't even recognize, from the other side of the rainbow.

'What the hell is that?' said Arthur.

'Advanced technology,' I said. 'And I mean *seriously* advanced. Even now, never mind back in Victorian times. There's no way humanity produced this.'

'And it's still working, after all these years?' Arthur stared, fascinated, at what I'd uncovered. 'This has to be the biggest story ever . . . Alien machines, hidden away from the world.'

'Malcolm's great secret,' said Penny. 'Not a prisoner or treasure . . . But how did he get his hands on something like this?'

'He must have found a crashed alien ship,' I said.

'Hold it,' said Arthur. 'That's a thing? That's something that actually happens?'

'Yes,' I said.

'Then why doesn't everyone know about it?' Arthur said loudly.

'Because there are very secret groups whose job it is to make sure people never know,' I said.

'I knew it!' said Arthur. 'But now I can't tell anyone! Typical of my luck . . . Do you work for one of these groups?'

'No,' I said. 'But I used to. Malcolm must have looted this technology from a crashed starship, thinking he could use the knowledge it contained. He used his transport business to bring it here and then built this house over it.'

'But then . . . why did he hide his prize away, behind this wall?' said Penny.

'Because it frightened him,' I said. 'I think the oppressive atmosphere we've been feeling all along is being broadcast by this tech. And it's been broadcast since Victorian times. Malcolm must have hoped a heavy stone wall would isolate it, but instead it just kept trying harder, until finally Malcolm and his family had no choice but to abandon the alien technology and the house.'

The awful feeling was suddenly worse. Penny cried out, and Arthur just vanished, like a candle blown out by a strong wind.

'Arthur!' I said loudly. 'Get back here! Don't let it drive you away, like it did your ancestors!'

Arthur reappeared, but I could barely make him out; it was as though he was having trouble remembering what he was supposed to look like.

Penny had both hands pressed to her head, covering her ears. Tears streamed down her cheeks, from the sheer horror of what she was being made to feel. And I was so furious at seeing her hurt that I attacked the wall with both hands, tearing away more stones to reveal yet more alien tech. The weird lights pulsed furiously, and a mad storm of voices filled my head. I punched the tech, and it shattered and fell apart.

The whole cellar shook. Stone after stone fell away, as though the alien technology was shrugging off what had hidden it for so long, and a whole wall of blazing metal and crystal appeared before me. Avalanches of stones were falling away everywhere, revealing alien tech on all four walls.

'This whole cellar is just one big mechanism!' I said, shouting to be heard over the raging clamour in our heads. 'It's a computer! We're standing inside an alien computer!'

A great voice issued from all four walls at once: a deafening, unbearably alien sound. More than just an inhuman voice speaking an unknown language; it didn't sound like anything a human being could produce or hope to understand. The sheer alien nature of it drove Penny to her knees, unable to cope with the impact of something so utterly other. Arthur flickered on and off, his face contorted by pain and horror. He was screaming soundlessly.

But I could still think clearly. Because for all the terrible noise in my head, there was something in the alien voice that I recognized. I shouted at it, straining my voice in the effort to be heard.

'Computer! Stop this! Stop trying to make contact! You have to shut yourself down, because you're damaging us! *This is an order!*'

The voice broke off, and there was a long moment of blissful silence. Arthur snapped back into focus, and Penny let her hands drop away from her ears. And then the alien technology lining all four walls just melted and ran away, in long pulsing streams. I grabbed Penny and pulled her away from the wall in front of us, until we were standing huddled together in the middle of the cellar. The molten wreckage heaved and steamed, and then just disappeared, dissipating rapidly into the air until not a trace of it remained.

The cellar was empty and still, and the stone walls surrounding us were merely walls. Only the collapsed rubble remained to show there had ever been anything else there.

'The atmosphere is gone,' Penny said breathlessly. 'It just stopped. I can't even remember what was so bad about it.'

'What the hell just happened?' said Arthur.

'We were standing inside some kind of artificial intelligence,' I said. 'It's been trying to communicate with us all along, but its thought processes were so different, so alien, that the human mind simply couldn't cope. We could only interpret what we were experiencing as horror and madness – an attack from outside.'

'That's what's been scaring people all these years?' said Arthur. 'A basic misunderstanding?'

'Isn't that always the way?' I said.

'Then why did it kill me?' said Arthur.

'It didn't,' I said. 'That was definitely one of the people upstairs. But I think it made use of your altered state to bring us down here so it could talk to us directly.'

'Then Harrow House really was haunted,' said Penny. 'By the thoughts of a trapped alien computer . . .'

'The AI must have been reaching out ever since Malcolm abandoned it,' I said. 'Searching for help. But the harder it tried, the worse it made people feel, filling their heads with images and concepts they couldn't hope to comprehend. Once I made the AI understand that, it self-destructed rather than do any more harm.'

'So there was something human about it,' said Penny.

'Human is as human does,' I said. I turned to Arthur. 'Harrow House will be just a house from now on. Your family can sell

it to our client and be done with it at last. The haunting – or,
more properly, the possession – is over.'

'A house with vacant possession!' Penny said happily.

I looked at her. 'You had to go there, didn't you?'

Penny grinned. 'Some things are just inevitable.'

'And now it's my turn to move on,' said Arthur. He suddenly
sounded very calm, almost serene. 'Everything's so clear. I
was only allowed to stay here to help bring you to this moment.'

'Do you know where you're going?' I said.

'No,' said Arthur. 'But . . . it feels like home.'

Penny realized what was happening. 'Goodbye, Arthur. I
wish I could have seen you.'

Arthur smiled at her and looked at me. 'Do you have any
idea why you were the only one who could see and hear me?'

Because I'm as alien as the computer, I thought but
didn't say.

'We'll probably never know,' I said.

He grinned. 'You should see the state of your aura . . .
Try to find out who killed me before you leave the house.'

'I'm on it,' I said.

Arthur turned and walked away, in a direction I could sense
but not name, and a moment later he was gone. I told Penny,
and she nodded.

'All the questions we could have asked him . . . Answers
Lynn and Freddie and Tom have been searching for their
whole lives.'

'To be fair,' I said, 'I don't think Arthur knew anything.'

'Perhaps he'll find out, when he gets where he's going,'
said Penny.

'It would be nice to think so,' I said. 'Come on . . . Let's
go back upstairs and tell the others the haunting is over.'

She slipped her arm through mine. 'Do you have any idea
which one of them killed Arthur?'

'Not really,' I said. 'It has to be something to do with what
happened before the seance.'

'I didn't see anything suspicious,' said Penny.

'Neither did I,' I said. 'But there has to be something . . .'

Penny shrugged. 'I thought Lynn handled the seance
really well.'

'She did,' I said. 'I was almost impressed.'

'Whether she's a fake or not, you have to hand it to her.'

'No . . .' I said. 'That's not it. Not quite.'

'What?' said Penny.

'I've just worked out what happened,' I said.

'But can you prove it?' said Penny.

'I need to study the recording one more time,' I said. 'And then I'll be able to explain to everyone exactly how it was done.'

'It's about time,' said Penny.

'Well,' I said. 'I have been a bit distracted.'

SEVEN

Death by Unnatural Causes

U p on the ground floor, the hallway seemed entirely peaceful. I tried to close the cellar door, but since I'd kicked its lock out, the door had decided it was sulking and didn't want to shut, so I just left it standing ajar.

'How did you know the computer would listen to you?' said Penny.

'Because I recognized the tech in the walls,' I said. 'I'd seen it before, in dreams of the ship that brought me to Earth.'

'You think the AI was built by your people?'

'It listened to me,' I said.

Penny shuddered. 'But it was so *alien*. If that thing was created by your people . . .'

'I know,' I said. 'What does that say about me?'

'No,' she said immediately. 'What you used to be, before you were human.'

'This is why I need to find the other crash survivor,' I said. 'So I can be sure of exactly what it is I'm turning my back on.'

Penny nodded slowly. 'What are we going to tell the others?'

'As little as possible, I should think.'

'We're going to have to tell them something!' said Penny. 'The whole feel of the house has changed. It's not as if we can blame everything we've experienced on mass hysteria.'

'I don't see why not,' I said. 'Mass hysteria is one of those marvellous expressions that doesn't actually mean anything, but sounds as though it does. So we can make it mean whatever we want it to. Which in this case amounts to: *It was all in your mind, nothing really happened, move along, nothing to see, mind how you go.*'

'They're never going to accept that,' said Penny. 'They'd take it as an insult to their intelligence, and I wouldn't blame them. And it practically guarantees they'll take their story to the media.'

'Let them,' I said. 'Whatever stories they tell will just add to the legend of Harrow House. And once our mysterious buyer moves in and nothing out of the ordinary happens, even the legend will start to fade.'

'All right,' Penny said resignedly. 'Let's go back and break the bad news to the others. Though I think I'll stand behind you while you do it.'

'Yes,' I said. 'It's time we told them how Arthur died.'

Penny looked at me sharply. 'You're certain about which one of them did it?'

'Pretty sure,' I said. 'I just need to check one more thing.'

'What?'

I grinned. 'Wait and see.'

I could hear Lynn, Freddie and Tom talking in the far room, as Penny and I approached the closed door. They were all chattering excitedly about the return of the grim atmosphere and its sudden disappearance, and what it all meant. I slammed the door open and strode in with Penny at my side. The others broke off from their arguing to study us suspiciously.

'Where have you been all this time?' said Lynn. 'We were worried!'

'You're the psychic,' I said reasonably. 'Shouldn't you have known what was happening?'

'Play nicely, darling,' Penny murmured.

'What have the two of you been up to?' said Freddie. 'Or shouldn't we ask?'

'Just taking care of business,' I said.

'You did something to settle the house, didn't you?' said Freddie. 'We all felt it go suddenly quiet, as though all the darkness had been exorcized. This house is clear now.'

'I wanted to say that!' said Lynn.

'Then you should have been quicker off the mark,' said Freddie.

'Penny and I have searched this house thoroughly,' I said. 'And we haven't been able to find anything of a supernatural nature. So our position is this: everything we experienced tonight was just the result of mood and atmosphere, shaped by our own personal beliefs and preconceptions.'

'You didn't find anything?' said Tom.

I raised an eyebrow at him, and he had the sense to stop talking. Freddie caught the look and frowned at me.

'What did you do to Tom? We've barely been able to get a word out of him since you sent him back to us.'

'I would have thought that was an improvement,' said Penny. 'Did you and Lynn make good use of his water bottle?'

'Turns out I didn't need it after all,' Lynn said airily. 'It was just the thought of needing to go, and not having anywhere to do it, that was getting to me. Once I had the option, I didn't want to any more. Isn't that always the way?'

'Penny and I are satisfied that Harrow House is not haunted, and never was,' I said sternly, bringing their attention back to me. 'And that is what we'll be saying in our official report. I'm sure our client will be very happy to hear that.'

'But Arthur died here!' said Freddie.

'Not because of the house,' I said.

'You can't be sure of that,' said Lynn.

'Yes, I can,' I said.

Lynn, Freddie and Tom sat back in their chairs, looking disappointed and not entirely convinced.

'We all saw and heard things,' Freddie said stubbornly. 'You can't dismiss all of it as mass hysteria!'

'That is a very useful term,' I said. 'I must be sure to include it in my report.'

'It's a shame Arthur didn't live long enough to know his family will finally be free of the stigma of owning the notorious Harrow House,' said Lynn. 'I think he would have liked that.'

Freddie glowered at me. 'How can you be so sure his death wasn't connected to the phenomena in this house?'

'Because there weren't any phenomena,' I said calmly. 'And that's official.'

Freddie sniffed loudly. 'We'll see about that. You wait till I write all of this up on my blog.'

'I think it's time we were leaving,' I said.

'We can't,' said Tom. 'The front door's still locked, remember?'

'Ah, yes,' I said. 'About that . . .'

I reached into my trouser pocket and brought out Arthur's house keys. Everyone looked at me speechlessly, including Penny. I smiled around me, entirely unmoved.

'You had the keys all along?' said Freddie. 'You took them? Why would you do something like that?'

'Because I didn't want anyone leaving the house until I could be sure who killed Arthur,' I said calmly. 'It was easy enough for me to lift the keys while I was checking his body for signs of life.'

Tom looked at me suspiciously. 'What made you decide that was necessary, so quickly?'

'Years of training,' I said.

'You kept us trapped here?' said Lynn, her voice thick with outrage. 'I've never been so frightened in my life! Who gave you the right to put us through that?'

'I'm security,' I said.

'Screw security,' said Freddie. 'We've been held prisoner in this house against our will, and . . . Wait a minute. You said you couldn't let us go until you knew who killed Arthur. Are you saying . . . that you know who did it?'

'Yes,' I said.

They all looked at me, and then at each other.

'Was it one of us?' said Tom.

'Of course,' I said. 'Who else could it be? Now then, before anyone leaves, I think we all need to take another look at the recording of the seance.'

'What's the point?' said Tom. 'It's not going to change, no matter how many times you watch it. That's the whole point of a recording.'

'But it's amazing what you can miss if you don't know what to look for,' I said. 'Set it up please, Tom.'

He nodded stiffly and moved over to his screen to work his laptop. Lynn and Freddie looked at him, and then at Penny and me.

'Yes, this really is necessary,' Penny said firmly. 'Trust Ishmael; he has excellent instincts when it comes to these things.'

'I don't think I want to go through this again,' said Lynn,

sticking her lower lip out sulkily. 'I think you take pleasure in watching that poor man die. Leave him alone! You're not going to see anything. The man is dead.'

'Which is why we have to go through this again,' I said. 'For his sake.'

'Got it!' said Tom. 'Where do you want me to start, Ishmael?'

'From when we all first sat down in the circle,' I said.

We stood together in front of the monitor screen, and I watched the familiar scene unfold with careful concentration. The others did too, sensing something important was happening, even if they couldn't tell what.

'That's it!' I said sharply. 'Tom, take it back to when Lynn started passing the cups of tea around.'

He did so, and we all watched closely as Lynn passed her hand over Arthur's cup in a blessing.

'Freeze it right there,' I said. 'Look closely, people. Do you see?'

They all leaned in, staring intently at the image on the screen.

'I'm sorry, Ishmael,' Tom said finally, 'but whatever it is you think you're seeing, I'm not seeing it. There couldn't have been anything wrong with the herbal tea, because we all drank it. So the tea couldn't have been the cause of Arthur's death.'

'Ah, but it was,' I said. 'Arthur didn't die of natural causes, and he wasn't frightened to death by the house. He was murdered in cold blood, using a trick carefully worked out in advance. Isn't that right, Lynn?'

There was a shocked silence, as everyone turned to look at Lynn. She stared back at us, as wide-eyed as a child behind her Goth makeup. Her mouth was trembling.

'You can't just say something like that!' she said loudly. 'You can't accuse me of murder, without any proof!'

'I have all the proof I need, right there on the screen,' I said. 'You murdered Arthur because he'd boasted he was going to expose you as a fake. He was going to prove to everyone that you were just another confidence trickster, right when you thought you were heading for the big time.'

Lynn met my gaze unflinchingly. 'Arthur wasn't the first to threaten me with that kind of nonsense. There are always going to be those who refuse to believe in things outside their experience or beyond their comprehension. Little people scared by a bigger world. And no one has ever been able to prove anything against me.'

'But Arthur was different,' I said. 'He did his research, and he talked to all the right people. He said he had hard evidence, and you believed him.'

'No,' said Lynn. 'No . . .'

'I was sure there was something odd about your behaviour leading up to the seance,' I said. 'And now I've had a chance to watch your movements carefully, I know exactly how you did it.' I looked at Freddie and Tom, who were listening to all of this with stunned fascination. 'Lynn passed her hand over each cup in turn, before she let us have our tea, but her hand lingered just that little bit longer over Arthur's cup. So she could surreptitiously drop something into his tea. Look at the screen, people. Look closely, and you can see the packet concealed in her palm. And what appears to be a fine powder falling into the cup. Anyone else might have missed it, but I have very good eyesight.'

I smiled easily at Lynn. 'You already told us you have a degree in organic chemistry. So you'd know exactly what to use: something that would be fast-acting as well as lethal. That's why you made such a fuss about us handing back the empty cups, just in case your poison had left a residue. But we'll see what an autopsy can turn up, once they've been told what to look for.

'Your constant insisting that all of us had an alibi, because we were all holding hands when Arthur died, never meant a thing, because Arthur had already been murdered. The darkness in the door was simply a lucky coincidence, something you could use to distract us from what had really happened.'

I stopped and waited for Lynn to say something. We were all staring at her now, but she just stood her ground and stared back. Freddie took a step forward. Lynn quickly started speaking as she took in the anger filling Freddie's face.

'It was just a blessing! I did it for all of you, to protect you from the forces in this house.'

'You killed him,' said Freddie. 'You killed my Arthur, my

lovely young man. I was just getting to know him, and you took him away from me.'

'I didn't!' said Lynn. 'Please, you have to believe me!' She turned suddenly to stab an accusing finger at me. 'It wasn't me; it was him! Ishmael killed Arthur!'

The sheer conviction in her voice was enough to make Freddie stop and turn to look at me.

'Why would Ishmael want to kill Arthur?' said Tom. 'He had never even met him before tonight.'

'How can we be sure of that?' said Lynn. 'He's security; who knows what a really good reporter might have discovered, which Ishmael couldn't afford for anyone else to know!'

Penny smiled at me. 'She's very good, isn't she?'

'Very good at what she does,' I said.

Lynn pressed on quickly, not wanting to lose the advantage. 'What do we know about either of them, really? They say they're security; but that could mean anything. We've all at least heard of each other, but Ishmael Jones . . . That doesn't even sound like a real name! He's already admitted he stole Arthur's keys, while the body was still warm, so he could keep us trapped in this awful place.'

'I still don't see why he'd want to kill Arthur,' said Tom.

'Then ask him!' said Lynn. 'Make him tell you!'

'No,' said Freddie, and everyone turned to look at her. She stared coldly at Lynn. 'It's not him. It was you.'

Lynn stared at her, shaken by Freddie's flat refusal to accept anything she'd said. 'Why won't you believe me?'

'Because you've been lying ever since you got here,' said Freddie. 'Little Miss Fake.'

'That's not true!' said Lynn. 'I've been feeling all kinds of things, ever since I entered this house.'

'Nothing the rest of us didn't feel,' Freddie said remorselessly. She turned to me. 'I don't know what you got up to while you were away, but you put a stop to what's been happening in this house. And you never once believed that the house killed Arthur. So given a choice between believing you and believing Lynn . . . well, it's no choice at all, really.'

Lynn bolted for the open door, catching everyone by surprise. She moved quickly, but I was always going to be

faster. I grabbed her by the shoulder and threw her back so
hard she fell to the floor. She scrabbled up on to her feet,
her face suddenly cold and dangerous. She started forward
again, and when I went to stop her, she threw a handful of
powder into my face. I squeezed my eyes shut instinctively,
and she darted past me. But Freddie was already there,
blocking her way to the door. I forced my eyes open just in
time to see Lynn throw herself at Freddie, and Freddie punch
Lynn in the face. Lynn's head snapped back, and she was
already unconscious before she hit the floor. Freddie scowled
down at her.

'That was for my Arthur.'

Penny was quickly there before me, scrubbing the powder
off my face with a handkerchief.

'Are you all right, Ishmael? Did the powder get in your
eyes? Did you breathe any of it?'

'I'm fine,' I said. 'I think you have to swallow it for it to
do you any harm.'

The stuff had no effect on me because I don't suffer from
all of humanity's weaknesses, but the others didn't need to
know that. I nodded to Freddie.

'Nicely handled.'

'She deserved it,' said Freddie. She looked at me steadily.
'Can you promise me she'll be properly punished for what
she did?'

'I can't be personally involved,' I said carefully, 'because
of who I work for. But I can make sure she's handed over to
the proper authorities, along with all the evidence needed
to convict her.'

Freddie was already shaking her head. 'That's not good
enough. Put her on trial? Can't you just see Lynn in front of
a jury? Without you there to back up the evidence, she'd find
some way to discredit it. She'd know all the right things to
say to charm a jury and wrap them round her little finger. She
would get away with murder, and I won't stand for that. Oh,
look . . . I do believe Lynn has died while we've been talking.'

I looked quickly at Lynn. She wasn't moving or breathing.
I knelt down on the floor beside her and checked for vital
signs, but there weren't any. Her eyes stared sightlessly out

of the dark makeup, and her black lips were stretched in a silent scream. I got to my feet again and looked steadily at Freddie.

'Aren't you going to try CPR or something?' said Tom.

'No point,' I said, not taking my eyes off Freddie. 'She's dead. And not a mark on her to show why.'

'How very strange,' said Freddie. 'Perhaps she died of fright.'

'You killed her!' said Tom.

'All I did was knock her on her arse,' said Freddie. 'Unless you think I killed her with my witchy powers.' She looked at me calmly. 'I think you'd be better off describing her death as natural causes, in your official report. Don't you, Mr Jones?'

'Why not?' I said. 'What's one more mystery in Harrow House?'

Freddie nodded. 'I liked Arthur. I really liked him.'

EIGHT
A Few Last Revelations

I n the morning, an unmarked ambulance arrived to take away Arthur's and Lynn's bodies. All part of the Organization's regular clean-up service. The local authorities would be informed later and told what the Organization decided they needed to know. As Tom and Freddie stood outside the front door of Harrow House with Penny and me, one of the stretcher bearers paused to murmur in my ear that they'd quietly wiped all of Tom's recordings, so there wouldn't be any evidence of my involvement. I nodded my thanks. Tom didn't notice.

Freddie watched them carry Arthur away, down the long gravel path and into the shadows of the overgrown garden. Only when he was completely out of sight did she turn round to look at the house.

'I'd hate to think some part of him might still be in there,' she said. 'The last ghost haunting Harrow House. That would be too much of an irony.'

'Trust me,' I said. 'There are no ghosts in Harrow House.'

Freddie searched my face and then nodded slowly. 'My sister Flossie will be here soon to pick me up. And lecture me, as usual, about wasting my life on this nonsense. Maybe she's right.'

'What will you do next?' Penny said politely.

'I'm giving up the whole white witch thing,' Freddie said flatly. 'I went too far at the end, though I can't bring myself to regret it. But I don't think I can afford to be tempted again. So . . . just a local historian from now on. Goodbye, Ishmael Jones and Penny Belcourt, or whoever you really are.'

She strode off down the gravel path and didn't look back once.

Tom cleared his throat awkwardly. 'I suppose I'd better be going too. The taxi I booked should be waiting. Are you sure there's no treasure here – maybe hidden away some-where, still waiting to be found?'

'Positive,' I said.

'Ah, well,' said Tom. 'That's the story of my life, right there.'

He insisted on shaking my hand and Penny's, before picking up his suitcases and walking off down the path. Penny and I stood together outside the empty house, enjoying the quiet morning. The garden seemed very peaceful in the rising light, and even the darkest shadows were completely still.

'I've been thinking,' said Penny.

'Good for you,' I said.

'That AI in the cellar dated all the way back to Victorian times. What were your people doing, visiting Earth all those years ago? I mean, I always assumed your ship crashing here was just an accident, but what if your people have been coming and going for centuries? What if they have some particular reason to be interested in humanity?'

'If I ever knew the answer to that, it's just one of the many things I've forgotten,' I said. 'Something else for me to ask the other survivor . . . Hold it. Someone's coming.'

Penny looked into the garden, straining her eyes against the shadows. 'I can't see anyone.'

'I heard the gates open,' I said. 'And then footsteps on the gravel path, heading our way.'

'You and your weird senses.'

'They do come in handy from time to time.'

'It could be the Colonel, turning up at last,' said Penny. 'Come to thank us for helping out at such short notice, and to tell us he's provided a lift back to our hotel, I hope.'

'It's not the Colonel,' I said.

'How can you be sure?'

'I know his footsteps,' I said. 'This is a much heavier man.'

'Alien,' Penny said fondly.

Mr Whisper finally emerged on to the open path – large as life and twice as impressive. He was still wearing his smart pinstripe suit, white leather gloves and yellow silk cravat. His dark shaven head gleamed in the early morning light. When he eventually joined us, his voice was the same harsh murmur.

'A very good morning to you both. Isn't it an absolutely splendid day? I thought I would make the journey in person, to thank you for your valuable assistance in this most delicate of matters.'

'The house isn't haunted,' I said.

'Was it ever?' said Whisper.

'Yes and no,' I said. 'You'll get all the details in our official report.'

I still hadn't decided exactly how much I was going to tell the Organization.

'The point is,' Penny said quickly, 'it's now perfectly safe for the buyer to go ahead. There's nothing about Harrow House that should concern him, or that might attract outside attention.'

'Excellent news,' said Whisper. 'I'll have the Colonel contact you as soon as he's free, Mr Jones, so the Organization can help you locate your missing person. And someone will be here soon, Ms Belcourt, to take the two of you back to your hotel.'

'I hope the buyer will be very happy here,' Penny said politely. 'A house like this has a lot of potential.'

'Though the cellar will need some repair work,' I said.

'It's a marvellous old house,' said Whisper. 'I'm sure I'll be very happy here.'

He bestowed one last beaming smile on us and then turned and walked away, disappearing back down the gravel path and into the shadows.

Penny looked at me. 'He was the buyer all along? Why didn't he tell us?'

'Because the Organization always likes to hold its secrets close to its chest,' I said. 'And perhaps because Mr Whisper didn't want us to know, in case things didn't work out well.'

'I think it all worked out very well, considering,' said Penny.

'We couldn't save Arthur,' I said.

'We found his murderer,' said Penny. 'Sometimes you have to settle for that.'

'And at least now we finally know someone high up in the Organization,' I said.

'What good does that do us?' said Penny.

'We know someone important, who owes us a favour,' I said patiently. 'And favours are currency in our line of work.'

'But can we trust him?' said Penny. 'The Organization keeps secrets from us, just as we keep secrets from them; it's not exactly the best foundation for group hugs and mutual support, is it?'

'I don't trust anyone,' I said. 'Apart from you, obviously.'

'Nice save, space boy.'

'You're welcome, spy girl. You don't have to trust someone to make a deal. You just have to make sure the end result is in everyone's best interests.'

Penny looked at me sharply. 'We've discussed the possibility that the other crash survivor could be someone who's already a part of your life. Keeping a watchful eye on you, for reasons of their own. Well, who'd be in a better position to do that than someone high up in the Organization?'

'You mean Mr Whisper?'

'Maybe all of this was just his way of introducing himself,' said Penny. 'Why else would he show up here in person?'

'So . . . I could be putting him in charge of trying to find himself,' I said. 'Interesting.'

'Well?' said Penny.

'Well, what?' I said politely.

'What are you going to do about it?'

'Nothing,' I said. 'It's just a theory.'

'But he sent you to investigate a house that contained AI built by your people! That has to mean something!'

I shook my head. 'I think I'd be able to tell if he was like me.'

'You've had a lot of experience when it comes to hiding your true nature from the world,' said Penny. 'Maybe he has, too.'

'There is one way to be sure,' I said.

'What?' said Penny.

'I could always punch him on the nose and see if he bleeds golden, like me.'

'I can see that going wrong in all kinds of ways,' said Penny.

I grinned at her. 'That's why I thought I'd leave it as a last resort.'

Penny slipped her arm through mine, and we stood together, looking out at the garden. I didn't feel in any particular hurry to go anywhere. It was a very lovely day.

'Something else did occur to me,' said Penny. 'Given that you were the only one who could see and hear Arthur, is it possible that what you were seeing wasn't actually his ghost at all, but just an image put in your mind by the AI? To bring you to it, so you could talk directly?'

I thought about it and then smiled.

'No,' I said. 'I don't believe that.'

Lightning Source UK Ltd.
Milton Keynes UK
UKHW010633250721
387663UK00002B/98